GOODBYE TRANSYLVANIA

A Young Man's Journey to Freedom

SAMUEL BISTRIAN

Goodbye Transylvania
A Young Man's Journey to Freedom
by Samuel Bistrian

Printed in the United States of America

ISBN 978-1-60791-000-8

www.xulonpress.com

Dedication

*This book is dedicated to my two lovely
grandmothers, "Baba" and "Bunica"
whose fragile-flames burnt out with unful-
filled desires. May your souls rest in
God's eternal peace.*

&

*To my precious angels and source of joy,
my daughters Ilona and Emma, my lovely
wife Alejandra, and to my amazing mother
Elizabeth, for all your tender care and
incessant generosity.*

Foreword

Where is the young man who dreams? How does the zeal of our youth so easily drain out of our lives? Like an aged cistern broken before its time so the creative and explorative natures of man have vanished into mere trickles of God's intent. Even amongst those who believe, I fear the stench of morbid replication has taken so deep a hold. These are the perils of our times. The paralyzing fear of dancing out of step has stopped many of us dead in our tracks. Hours, days and months go by with inactivity towards the causes true to God and our own destinies alike. It is through these eyes of seeing that I met and recognized Samuel Bistrian. From the first encounter I could sense the greatness of spirit, determination and boldness. I knew he loved God and that he would never back down from doing what is difficult if he believes it is the right thing to do. Of all the attributes I respect about Samuel this one has encouraged me time and time again more than any other.

This book is simply a tribute to the human spirit unvanquished by modernization and conformity.

Read it and remember when you dared to dream. Look back and realize that as a child God gave you desire, natural characteristics and leanings. These attributes are a flint to be used for sparking a fire. Let the fire ignite your own passions to create and make your mark on this world. The greatest tragedy of all is to finish the race, intact, amidst the pack and realize you were in the wrong event. You are the son or daughter of the Creator and as such your identity begs, in fact dictates, that you live free and soar. So read this tribute to freedom and soar with the author's testimonies of God's faithfulness.

I declare to you the reader and the spirits of the air; "We are not robots. We shall not go quietly into the night as mere shadows of men and women. We shall create as our creator created. We shall dance the dance. We shall sing with our own voice. We will live free."

Israel Lambert
September 2008

Preface

From pre-Revolutionary Romania to communist-ruled Cuba, my life's journey has taken me many places. I was born in Benesti, Romania, as the ninth of twelve children. Early on in my childhood I felt a strong passion for traveling, but my desire was not satisfied until I was able to escape Benesti.

This book is my voyage from a remote village in the mountains of Transylvania during communist rule, to the difficult transition most immigrants face when emigrating to America. Eventually my childhood dreams would become realities as I would get the opportunity to travel the world.

From the slums of a third world to the glories of democracy, communism to capitalism, and tyranny to liberty: I ventured to a much better life, to freedom and opportunity. And though nothing came easy, I was able to find strength and courage to move forward, and hope for a brighter future.

This book was written as I traveled through four different continents. It's simply humanity's fight for liberty and the guiding faith that led me to finding my destiny. From inner city Chicago, to Tennessee, then Dallas and beyond, my family and I learned hard lessons, but we never lost our gratitude and faith in God or this country.

And our gratitude for the opportunities given, translated into our desire or even a moral obligation to share with others and to give back to the world in truly remarkable ways.

Samuel Bistrian
November 29, 2008

part
ONE

Difficulties & Dilemmas

1

Independence Day

The new millennium came swiftly and the world never ended. The years were passing, knowledge was increasing, and people were running to and fro more than ever.

It was the Fourth of July, and fortunately freedom still rang in our great nation! At long last I had become an adult and for me, life was just beginning. Just a few months earlier I had graduated high school. The words of one of my teachers still echoed in my mind, loud and clear, "It's your opportunity to make a difference, to live the dream. Do it while you still can."

For me Independence Day was celebrated twice a year; once in July with the American nation that adopted me, and again, on December 25, the day that marked the end of tyranny in my former country of Romania.

While Americans across the world were getting ready for barbeques, picnics, and fireworks celebrations, I was preparing for a road trip.

The beginning of the new millennium meant the beginning of a new chapter in my life. My ambitions of becoming a realtor were dissolved by my lack of impetus and enthusiasm, and my plans to serve in the military were swayed by the fear that America would soon be going to war, and by my admitted cowardice.

Ever mindful of my privilege of being a citizen in the land of great opportunities, I decided to do some soul-searching and discover my true destiny. Sure, we all have dreams and aspirations, but the difficulty is listening to our hearts, seeing beyond our horizons and chasing those dreams.

One thing I knew definitely. I was not going to allow myself to live a mediocre life. Something within me needed to be revived and stimulated. I was born to fly, to run free and to explore the world. It was time to leave home, but my direction wasn't clear. I pondered the thought of following the path of my eight older siblings: move to Texas, and enroll in this "life-changing school" they enthusiastically talked about. It sounded good, but I wasn't sold on it yet.

I knew, however, that my time in Tennessee had expired and that I was destined for something else, for some greater purpose. Nearly ten years had flown by, and I felt trapped in the same stale, sterile environment. My life was losing color, and I was ready to break free from the familiarity to which I'd grown so accustomed. With high school behind me, it was time to rekindle my passion for travel.

2

My First Journey

It all began when I was a toddler taking my first steps, walking alone through the back yard, full of corn stacks and hay bundles. Mom and Grandma would look for me anxiously, fearing that I was in the barn or the pig stall, or worse that I had fallen into the fish pond or one of the wells Dad had recently dug. It's not that Mom was irresponsible or careless. She just had too many other obligations and tasks that kept her from constantly keeping her eyes on me. The older boys were out in the pasture and the girls were in the fields. Dad was working in the mines, and Mom was left with Grandma to cook, wash diapers and care for newborn Danny, Emmanuel and me, both of us toddlers.

As I grew from a toddler to a young boy I was dubbed "the curious wanderer" because of my continued curiosity. Often Mom would call me in for supper, but I wouldn't hear her. I was off again, this time discovering our village, which was about a kilometer in length. Upon my return, she would say, "Esurum, my son, where have you been?" *Esurum* is a Romanian term used to describe one who constantly wanders off on a personal journey.

Mind you, I did have eleven siblings. For me to constantly be the last one in, meant one of two things; either, I hated mealtimes and being with my family, or I just loved being outdoors, exploring away from home. The latter rings truer, which is ironic, considering I was the only child out of twelve born at home.

When I started school the problem persisted. I was just six years old, the year was 1988, and I was beginning my first year in elementary school. It was a cold, but beautiful early spring day in March, and we took a small walking excursion to the mountains surrounding our village to pick "*ghiocei.*" Ghiocei, also known as snow drops, are beautiful, white, spring flowers, with a delightful scent. They're the first flowers to bloom in the spring even before the snow melts, indicating that at long last, winter is over.

Every spring in Romania we celebrated two holidays. The first one, "*Martisor* (Ladies Day)" is celebrated the first of March and the other, "Mother's Day" the eight of March. It's typical for boys to give fresh flowers to their mothers, preferably ghiocei, and to their girlfriends, *martisoare*, a talisman object consisting of a jewel or small decoration like a flower, an animal, or a heart, tied to a red and white string.

That special day we hiked to the edge of the mountains where we knew we would find the beautiful ghiocei. Altogether we were about ten kids, not including the professor. We each spread out looking for the beautiful flowers.

After collecting as many as my little tight fist could hold, I decided to enter the forest and climb up the mountain to see if I could see what was on the other side. I always believed that once I reached the summit there would either be a big black wall or an endless sea, and I wanted to see it for myself. So I climbed away, while the other students were collecting their flowers and making snow balls out of the slush that remained. I climbed and climbed, but the top was far away... I was not thinking of the wild boars, deer, bears, bobcats, or any of the other wild animals who inhabited the Carpathian Mountains. I would've kept climbing, but I got too tired and cold.

Upon my return, which was at the complete opposite side of the village, I encountered a few shepherds clothed in sheepskin and big rubber boots. They lived in small tents on the outskirts of the village with their dogs, and took care of the government flocks. One of the shepherds led me to the schoolyard where the other kids were running free and playing, while the professor was still out searching for me. One of my classmates told me that I was in trouble, but the rest were too distracted to say anything. I wasn't gone for long, but it was certainly enough to enrage the professor.

Within a short while he returned, but didn't act surprised to see me. It was as if he knew that I would find my way back. With a wry smirk, he ordered me to step in front of the class and tell everyone where I had been. *"Yay!"* I figured, *"This is my opportunity to tell everyone that I saw the end of the forest."*

A few seconds passed and while I was still telling my story he interrupted, "Can you hold your fingers together for me?" "Turn them upwards," he said as he scanned the classroom with an expression that cast an air of intimidation on all his students. He asked that I continue to face the class as he walked behind me, reached to his desk, and grabbed a long wooden ruler. He took the ruler and with the sharp edge began to batter my finger tips until they were blue and swollen, my fragile nails denting by the impact of the force. I slightly pulled back, my soft cry erupting into a loud sob, but he continued. "The more you pull back, the longer and harder I'm going to hit," he threatened.

He was a true communist, soulless and daunting, and he wanted to make a public spectacle out of me. He wanted to teach a lesson to the other students. "I'm going to tell my Daddy," I shouted as I ran for the door. He didn't bother chasing me.

I arrived home but received little consolation from Mom, and from Dad chastisement for leaving school. They didn't want a spoiled child, but this guy had crossed the line. They feared him. We were peasants, after all, and he was an educated professor working for the communist government. At that time, under that regime, anyone in a position of authority was to be feared and esteemed.

How times have changed... But the wounds, the trauma, and the oppression I still remember.

I remember the fear, the hunger, and the cold. I remember it all like it was yesterday.

Daily life was arduous and travel was not easy. I always wanted to get away, to flee to the city, but I was limited. We owned a horse and an old motorcycle which Dad used to get to work. Our two means of transportation were used strictly for business. For my family and other residents of *Benesti* (my village) travel was limited as there was only one not very reliable bus in the morning and the same unreliable bus in the evening. Two of my older sisters were employed in the city. One had just married and lived in the city with her husband.

On a hot summer day in 1989, continuing my quest for freedom, I orchestrated a plan to escape our village and see what else was out there. I took one younger and one older brother with me, and we made our way to the unofficial bus stop, which was just in front of the village discotheque. I was seven years old and strongly dedicated to adventure, while Danny was barely six, and Emanuel was going on nine. Danny was the quiet, somber type who tagged along and never really voiced his opinions. Emanuel was more analytical and cautious, but he figured this was a good opportunity to escape our village for the day.

As soon as the bus arrived, we were there, ready for our grand opportunity. In those days we had no worries, nor thought about the potential dangers or consequences of our travels.

To be gone from home for most of the day was not at all unusual. Responsibility came at an early age and everyone had a daily assignment. Oftentimes the younger children would take the animals to the pasture to be fed from dusk till dawn, while the older children worked in the fields, tilling the soil and harvesting the family or government-owned land. No matter what the daily chores were, everyone in the family had to participate.

In the summer we harvested the crops. In autumn we had to prepare for the winter by chopping wood in the forest. After spending all day in the woods with an ax and a few knives, we'd return home, in single file, beginning with the oldest, who was fifteen, to the youngest, who was five, each of us carrying a bundle of firewood proportionate to our size. In the winter, we had big frozen pumpkins reserved for feeding the swine. My brothers and I would have the pleasure of splitting them and removing the seeds until we could no longer feel our fingers, they were so icy cold. The seeds were roasted and the pumpkins were to be food for the swine all winter long. Every year before Christmas we would identify the largest hog and Dad would mercilessly slit its throat. This was the moment I dreaded most. I would go into the house and with a pillow over my head I would sing and shout trying hard to drown out the squealing and screeching that many times drove me to tears. Even when Mom would cut the head of a duck or a goose I sometimes cried. I always had a strong heart, but sensitive nevertheless. My brothers, Danny and Emmanuel, on the other hand enjoyed the slaughter of our annual Christmas hog. In fact, Danny couldn't wait for the day when Dad would let him do the job.

Once it was over, Emanuel would call for me to help cover the hog with hay, before Dad would torch it. Then, the incision, it was gross... the smell and the entrails made me ill. We weren't allowed to be fastidious, we had no choice, as the hog had to last the entire winter and spring. Therefore, we utilized everything. The hog's tongue, ears, and tail, would be used for making a gelatin dish that I never came to enjoy. With the stomach, we made a famous tripe soup, with the legs, a prosciutto, the cleaned intestines and what remained would be used to make a variety of sausages which Dad would later smoke and cure in the attic. Occasionally I would get so hungry that I would sneak up to the attic, take a bite of the hanging sausages and blame it on the rats. The lard of the hog was the most interesting... Some was fried then frozen and used as bread spread, sprinkled with paprika, which made for a quick, tasty, and very unhealthy snack. The rest of the lard was used to make soap which was used to wash clothing, since we had no detergent. Village life was active and challenging, but very dynamic. When there wasn't anything to be done at our house, a very infrequent occurrence, we would help our neighbors. We were a small community. Therefore, it was common for everyone to care for one another.

Back to the story I was relating earlier... Danny, Emanuel, and I left the house this particular day, like any other day, assuming that Mom and Dad would never notice. But this day was different. The city of Ineu was about two hours away and the only other trip I'd taken prior to this day that I could remember covered the same route, but was a short few minutes from our village. Still, my recollection did not quiet my nerves and unease. I was somewhat scared of the unknown, but I could not contain my curiosity and excitement of going to the big city. We managed to sneak onto the bus unnoticed by mingling in with other passengers and off we went.

The old bus squeaked and grunted as we drove away and the ride seemed much bumpier even than on our horse and cart. We sat all the way in the back, crammed in a corner trying to conceal our faces from the angry-looking busman. He was a sloppy and careless driver, hitting every pot hole on that dusty dirt road. But nothing mattered more to us than going to the city. The two hours felt like an eternity until we arrived at our destination. I remember looking around and seeing what appeared to be an entirely different world. Communism did not offer a whole lot. However, Ineu and its people were completely different from what I knew. They spoke, dressed and lived differently. The pace and the lifestyle were completely different from ours. Businesses, cars, and buildings more than one story tall were all too much for me to fathom. People were everywhere, and selling anything they could. I was overwhelmed by the hordes of people at the bus station. Vendors were selling various used wares, street snacks, vegetables and fruits; one selling sunflower seeds and another *langosh* (a fried Romanian pastry). People were selling anything attainable in this third world country.

It was an incredible journey for a young boy coming from a village of eighty people to arrive in a city of more than 10,000. It was much more than I could have ever visualized. We were young kids with no money, no sense of direction, but full of courage, and we felt ready for anything.

Assuming that everyone knew our sister, we asked stranger after stranger for directions to her house. We never expected to encounter so much commotion and confusion. The only thing we actually knew was that she ran a langosh and juice shop on the main street, somewhere near the town square.

I remember being extremely cautious of the "gypsies." As we tirelessly walked, trying to navigate our way toward the town square, we were careful to keep a great distance from anyone who had even the slightest appearance of a gypsy.

As I always had a good sense of direction, I led the way, Emmanuel was next to me, looking out for the gypsies, and Danny was right behind us muttering random observations. "There's one who keeps looking at us," Emmanuel pointed, as we approached an area where old women, who looked like witches, dressed in long black dresses and black head coverings were selling sunflower seeds. We entered small shops, crisscrossed the streets, and did everything we could to avoid the gypsies that we thought were following us.

In those days we heard many stories of gypsies stealing young kids, abusing them, and using them as beggars or even selling them for a profit. True or untrue, we didn't want to take chances.

After wandering for a few hours, we finally found my sister's house. Her husband welcomed us with hot langosh and pineapple juice. I had never even seen or tasted a pineapple before, but the exotic juice was savory and refreshing on that scorching hot day.

Later my sister showed up carrying a brown paper bag. "What a surprise! It's so nice to see you here. How did you find us?" she inquired, as she put the bag down and gave us all hugs.

I wanted to know what was in the bag. Part of me believed that she knew we were coming and went out to buy us toys, but those were just the wishful thoughts of a child. In the bag was a loaf of dark stale bread and half a dozen eggs, for which she had waited in line all morning long. It was obvious that the city was much different than our village.

We told them stories of how we escaped Benesti and how the gypsies in the city were watching us. They just laughed and offered us more food. We spent a few hours admiring their home and stuffing ourselves with langosh and juice. It was seldom we got to eat like this. Most times the food ran out before our appetites were satisfied and we would go to sleep hungry. This time, with plenty of langosh before our eyes, we made sure to indulge in all that they offered.

We asked many bizarre questions about everything we observed. "Why do you have to wait all day in line for potatoes? Where does the water go when it's flushed down the toilet? How does it get there?" We were so intrigued by everything and curious to know as much as we could about all that we encountered.

Just as they thought they had answered all of our questions, I asked, "Do you have a television, does everyone?" I really wanted to see cartoons but I would have to wait for another time.

Time quickly passed and before we knew it, it was time to return and take the evening bus back to the village. I asked my sister if we could take some langosh and juice for Mom and Dad, so they'll forgive us for leaving without permission. It wasn't a problem. My sister's husband accompanied us to the station, which seemed so much closer than when we arrived. This time we were able to get on the bus without any worries.

On the way home we passed towns, communes, and villages. My imagination soared with thoughts of escaping to the city forever. As I sat on that bus looking toward the red sky as the sun was setting, I couldn't help but wonder what an alternative life would be like.

This was my first official trip to the city and little did I know that this was but a small glimpse of what would follow in my life. The same breathtaking experience of arriving to a new city, a new country, or even a new continent would be repeated over and over throughout my life.

3

Romania

(The Departure)

I remember coming home one miserable and rainy day in the late spring of 1989, crying, stressed and frustrated. It had been a difficult and bitter year already and poverty had reached an all time high in our village and in our country. Just a month earlier, I was in our back yard trying to skate on the frozen pond when suddenly the ice broke from underneath me and I slipped in. I was lucky enough to survive, but I lost one of my only shoes.

I had just turned seven years old and I didn't get a birthday present. Instead, I was given more responsibility. There was a cute girl at school, but I was always too shy to talk to her. When I finally mustered the courage to walk over to her during recess, I was humiliated by an older bully who spat in my face.

Nothing seemed to be going right in my personal world or the world around me and it was getting worse

27

by the day. I was in the pasture watching over the family cow and practicing my handwriting. As night fell, like the other villagers, I had to walk our milk machine home to the barn. This cow was no ordinary cow. She was stubborn and often ran off into the corn fields. I wanted to avoid the hollow woods, so I took the long path by the cherry valley overlooking the mountains surrounding our village. Just before entering town, a dog began barking by the nearby cemetery, and the cow shot off like an angry bull in Pamplona. I ran and ran, chasing her as far as I could, but eventually lost sight of her. I knew what awaited me at home if I returned without her, but I was too frightened and exhausted to continue my pursuit, so I decided to take my chances and pay the price later.

As I timidly approached my house with my shoes smothered in mud and my clothes drenched by the rain, I noticed something unusual. There was a white Dacia in front of our house, which immediately softened my anxiety. To my surprise and with tears in my eyes I arrived to a cheerful home.

The driver of the white car was a family relative from the United States. She was visiting and exploring the possibility of helping us move to "America." Excited about the refreshing news, my parents did not even think of reprimanding me. Instead, I was quickly forgotten, much like the cow. They were too busy with more important business matters to discuss.

This was a time in Romania when it was extremely difficult for anyone to go to the United States, and for a family of fourteen, nearly impossible. The revolution had just ended, but that didn't make matters easier. The country was in utter pandemonium and it would take divine providence to create such a miracle. There was so much confusion and instability. Nobody knew who would take the helm, and lead our country to a brighter future.

We needed someone loyal and sympathetic to the people's needs, someone unlike Nicolae Ceausescu who suppressed us for twenty-five years and attempted to brainwash us with his empty rhetoric. Ceausescu was consistently out of touch with the Romanian people and with reality. He actually thought he had created a Utopia. He believed Romania was experiencing its best years as a nation, and that it was far more advanced then any of the other Eastern Bloc Nations.

He and his family were living the high life in large, luxurious palaces with everything anyone could ever dream of. Meanwhile, the people were living in small (barrack-style) apartments, dying of starvation, suffering from lack of good health care, and constantly experiencing electricity shortages.

The Romanian people were fed up. They were tired of the communist propaganda, but they were afraid to speak out, knowing that if they did, there would be severe consequences.

There was a Hungarian Priest in Timisoara, however, who decided to speak and let the world know how he felt about the communist regime. It was not long before the secret police began to harass him. It didn't stop there. The police took away his apartment and threatened to evict him for his criticism.

On December 16, 1989 a group of students joined in his defense and the defense of religious freedom staging a protest. The police responded by beating, harassing, and spraying the protesters with tear gas. But all the tactics used by the police didn't quiet the angry marchers. The next day the protests resumed and the roar of the revolution got louder and stronger as thousands marched around Timisoara crying for an end to communism.

I once heard a saying by a student of revolution, "Revolt is the result of hungry citizens." This statement proved to be true in both a literal and metaphorical sense. The Romanians were as hungry as they had ever been. Our country, at that time, was considered to have the lowest living standards of any of the Eastern Bloc Nations. Poverty had reached an all time high.

Ceausescu was departing Bucharest for a visit to Iran, leaving the unrest to his wife Elena, and his subordinates. Upon returning from his trip on December 20, the situation in Timisoara grew tenser and the news of the revolution had spread to the outside world. The next day, attempting to restore order and authority, Ceausescu addressed an assembly of more than 100,000 people, condemning the uprising in Timisoara.

Once again, he proved to be out of touch with the people. He totally misread their mood. The people were apathetic and there was hardly any cheering. The speech turned into chaos as protesters interrupted with jeers and anti-communist slogans, turning the capital in to a complete state of turmoil. Ceausescu, out of desperation, tried to prevent the radio and television media from broadcasting the news, but to no avail. It was too late now. More than seventy-six percent of the country got a glimpse of what was happening.

Eventually the majority joined the revolution. Seeing this, Ceausescu went all out employing tanks, soldiers, and anti-terrorism troops, allowing the full use of force to regain control. Many of the protesters were beaten, stabbed, arrested, and killed, but the battle continued. Ceausescu's plan to disperse the military throughout the country backfired. The military eventually joined the anthem of protesters, shouting "Down with the dictator!"

When Ceausescu realized that the crowds were tenacious in their pursuit of freedom and that the people had turned against him, he tried to escape. He took his wife and went into hiding. Within a short while, they were discovered and brought to trial.

What irony in that on Christmas Day in 1989, the whole world watched as these same military soldiers who received order from Ceausescu just days earlier, tied his hands behind his back and led him and his wife to an orange wall where a firing squad awaited them.

The people of Romania were free at last, but the unrest continued for days after the execution. Many had no idea what the future would bring. They were skeptical of who would take charge. There was a lot of confusion and chaos leading into the New Year, but at the same time, the people of Romania were able to breathe a sigh of relief after nearly a quarter century of Nicolae Ceausescu's policies.

Emotions filled the country. Many people went out in the streets crying tears of joy, shouting, and giving each other gifts. Since there was only one television set in our entire village, most of us knew very little about the situation. Most of the villagers were out in the streets trying to figure out what would happen to the country, to the people, and to the state-owned land that was the object of their daily toil.

Everyone had a tale to tell. Some doubted Ceausescu had been executed. Others suspected a worse dictator would replace him. There was a lot of speculation, but as the weeks passed, we, as a family, became less concerned with the country's predicament and more focused on getting to America.

We eagerly waited and prayed for our visas to be approved. Meanwhile, my parents were making all the necessary preparations for us to leave. They sold paprika, house artifacts, a tractor that we had just bought for farming, and our livestock to have some extra cash to help us along the way. The most heart-breaking thing for me was, having to sell our horse Monica, which had been in the family ever since I was a baby. Monica was undoubtedly the best horse we've ever owned.

I remember taking her to the pasture one day. I must have been six or seven and just learning to ride. She galloped so fast that I lost my grip and fell off of her onto the green grass below. Somehow my foot got caught and I landed right between her legs. She nearly plowed her left rear leg into my rib cage, but, being the cautious and caring horse that she was, she hopped right over me. Then she knelt down to check on me, rubbing her head against my body to make sure I was OK.

With all the packing, planning, and preparing around the house, Monica sensed we were up to something. It's as if she knew we would be departing even before the departure was confirmed. I noticed her sorrow and her pain by the sadness displayed in her eyes and it made me sadder, but there was nothing I could do.

To everyone's surprise, permission from the embassy was granted, and Bucharest awaited our arrival. Miraculously, we were one of very few families to have this opportunity, considering the disorder of the country at that time. During that time Bucharest was the only city in Romania with an international airport. It was also the capital where we would get our visas and our passports.

The day before departing for Bucharest was a day of both joy and sadness. Family, friends, and neighbors gathered at our home for a final reunion. Most houses in Romania have a courtyard enclosed by a large gate. There in our courtyard we were joined by more people than I've ever seen in Benesti.

There were saxophones, accordions, and harmonicas playing sad departure songs as we ate, laughed, cried, and embraced each other. Who knew if, when, and where we would ever see each other again? We maximized the day and savored our last moments together by staying up until the wee hours of the morning.

The next day quickly arrived and we were dragging from lack of sleep. A few cars were needed to transport us to the nearest train station. It was a cold and windy autumn day and there was no shelter at the train station to protect us from the cold weather. We snuggled together and waited for the train to arrive.

Finally after what felt like forever we heard the whistling in the distance. As we were getting ready to board our hearts broke with emotions as we realized this was the final moment. We said our last goodbyes to Emily and "Bunica," Mom's mother, who accompanied us to the train station a few villages away.

Bunica was the sweetest person alive, often visiting us with candy, nuts, and fruits. I don't recall her ever showing up at our doorstep empty handed. We would have loved for her to come with us, especially since my aunt, her other daughter, had recently passed away. However, it wasn't possible to bring her and we had to leave her behind to be cared for by others.

Through the stained windows of the train we could see her waving and waving with one hand, flowers in her other hand, and tears streaming down her wrinkled and delicate face as we slowly pulled away. That was the last time I would see her.

Bucharest

The year was 1990 and we safely arrived in our nation's capital. It was bitterly cold and we were emotionally drained by our departure and exhausted from the cramped, long, and noisy train ride. We were stuck in a small compartment of a communist train for more than ten hours, while babies were crying, men were drinking Tuica (a Romanian moonshine), and chain smoking Kent cigarettes. Thinking back on that trip, it was awful and toilsome for the entire family, but we had no other alternative.

Bucharest was still feeling the aftermath of the Revolution. I looked around and nothing impressed me. Yes, the buildings were bigger and the city was obviously bigger and busier than any other city I had ever seen, but the residue of brokenness lingered in the streets. It was dirty, disorganized, and the people's somber faces reflected the city's nature. The city was like a broken machine that the people wanted to piece back together but were hesitant to begin.

Many had lost their lives fighting for freedom, and many children were neglected, left to be orphans. The feeling of hopelessness and despair was evident everywhere.

What had the revolution accomplished? The new Romania needed much more than vague promises. It needed solutions. The country was afraid of the future. It needed faith. I thought of America and knew that nothing would compare to it.

From communism to liberation, what was next? Where do you begin? Rebuilding mentally, emotionally, and economically was going to be a long and arduous process. We were fortunate to leave this mess, but what about our people? What about their future?

Rome (a foreshadowing)

The two weeks we spent in Bucharest were overwhelming. I still could not believe the enormous changes that we were so rapidly experiencing. Imagine what America was going to be like! So much was happening so fast, I had no idea what to expect. The future seemed obscure.

Two weeks after our arrival in Bucharest we were off to the airport and on to America, but not before making a small stopover in Italy. This was my first time in an airport and my first opportunity to enter an aircraft. The minute I set foot in the airport I felt a switch in my emotions. I was suddenly in good spirits. It was as if there was a latent connection that felt very familiar and fulfilling. Looking through the dust-stained windows of the Henry Coanda International Airport, the Tarom Boeing 737 was immense and seemed bigger than any Airbus 380 of today. I could not believe my eyes!

I remember loving planes all my life. As a kid I always wanted to become a pilot so that I could soar freely over the world. I loved gazing in the blue skies searching for airplanes. Seeing one in a blue moon, the size of my pinky finger flying over the village, was as special as Christmas to us kids. The other kids and I would run throughout the village, chasing it until it would finally fade away and all that remained were lines of smoke in the distance.

How monumental this moment was! I finally got to see one up close. I wondered why the windows were so small and marveled at what was inside this amazing aircraft. We were all so eager to just board and fly, but we had to wait what seemed like forever to accomplish all that takes place at an airport. To a child, passport control, checking bags and security feels endless. I was too young and too excited to have that kind of patience, but I had no choice. Constraint was the most respected word in our home.

Mom had sat us all down and reminded us of the conversation we had before leaving Benesti. "Now, this is just the beginning of our trip, let's all behave and watch out for one another." We had our family government in place. The oldest was twenty-two years old and the youngest was two. The two oldest daughters were in charge of looking out for me, Danny and Emmanuel. The two younger ones were in charge of caring for the babies, along with my Mom. And the two older brothers were to help my Dad with the suitcases. "Wait and see what awaits you in America if you don't behave," threatened my Dad. "Order and discipline," were his favorite words and now that we were away from the village, he made sure to give us a double-dose of them, for fear of losing his grip on us.

Finally, we all boarded through the jet way, which I thought was a tunnel within the airplane. When I finally entered the plane I realized it was much smaller than what I had imagined. We took our seats which reeked of cigarettes and other unusual odors. The flight attendants took time to help each one of us individually fasten our seatbelts and explain the procedures within the plane. The level of excitement was peaking. When the jets were turned to full throttle and the airplane finally left the ground my heart was ready to explode. This was the best feeling in the world!

I remember looking out of the window and seeing large ships gradually getting smaller as we flew over and away from the Black Sea. Eventually everything would disappear as we ascended higher and higher into the blue skies. I thought that if we climbed any higher we would see stars and planets. It was a blissful experience! I felt like we were as close to heaven as we'd ever been. Every moment of the flight was exciting and memorable.

Upon our arrival in Rome, I had another astounding experience. In fact, I had flashbacks of my first trip to the city just a little over a year ago. But this time it was splendid and my senses were on overload.

The architecture, history, culture and food were paradise. It was so much different and better than anything I had ever known.

Being waited on and served was so humbling. The food was something I had never tried before, and my taste buds were acclimating to so many new and delightful flavors. Delicious would be an understatement.

The people were loud, friendly, and warm. The cheerful ambiance, the excitement and smiling faces all around us were so different from the somber and depressed mood of Romania.

As we were eating I looked over at Mom as she was feeding Abel, the baby of the family, who at the time was only two years old. She had a tender look of gratitude on her face. I can still remember the words that she would often repeat, "God has blessed our family and has a great purpose for all of us." At eight years old I was beginning to see the blessing unfold.

At that time I couldn't thoroughly understand destiny and I didn't know the true meaning of purpose, but just the sound of it gave me hope. It allowed me to realize that there was more out there and that we were destined for something greater. Mom had the faith to see it while we were yet in Benesti. I was just beginning to see it.

It was sad leaving Romania. Leaving my dear grandmothers and my sweet sister Emily behind was heartbreaking. Nevertheless, escaping a hopeless world to build a future where there were endless opportunities would be our reward.

Rome was just a small glimpse of that life and the liberty it offered. It gave us a small taste of how we could live and what we could accomplish and we were left with great anticipation for what was soon to follow. After our two-week-stay, we were more eager than ever to see what this new world would be like. America, here we come!

4

New to America

We arrived in Chicago on a cold November night. The date was November 29, 1990, and it was a special day for all of us, but especially for Peter and Daniela, the only siblings who were born on the same day. It was their birthday and what a long birthday it was, considering all the time zones we crossed.

There we were, at the great Chicago O'Hare Airport looking around with curiosity and disbelief that we had finally made it. Wow! What a great feeling! We were finally in America. None of us spoke a word of English. We didn't know where to go and who to find. We stood around in amazement at everything we saw, until help found us. The airport was so big, bright, and clean. It was beautifully decorated for the holidays and gentle Christmas melodies were heard everywhere. It was wonderful!

We were dressed in our best clothing, but even our best clothes were ragged. They had been passed down from older siblings and were reserved for special occasions. I remember looking around in awe at everything I saw. I felt so out of place, and I couldn't see how we would ever amalgamate with this newfound culture.

The relative who had sponsored us and provided the invitation never made it to the airport, but she sent a family of five brothers to pick us up. They didn't have any trouble locating us. We were like a group of timid doves surrounded by bold eagles. It was hard to miss us. With big smiles they confidently approached us and introduced themselves.

They looked very wealthy compared to us, although they weren't. They were an average middle class family who had come to America, just like us. I still recall melded feelings of excitement and inferiority as they suddenly embraced us and welcomed us to America. They all had jean jackets and big smiles on their faces. To me they were the coolest guys I had ever met. For years all I wanted was a jean jacket.

In order to accommodate us all we were split into two different houses. The guys went to one house, the girls and my parents to another. This was just temporary until we could find our own place.

We arrived at a beautiful house in what I later realized was one of Chicago's nicer neighborhoods. That was the night I was introduced to "pizza." This was not just any ordinary pizza I was told, this was Chicago-style-pizza. But I never would have been able to tell the difference. I had no idea what pizza was! I had never even heard the word pizza before, not even in our stay in Italy. That night I ate pizza like it was an American delicacy. What a treat it was for all of us!

We would spend the coming days learning to play video games, which to us was a phenomenon. It was Nintendo and Atari non-stop. At night we watched shows like *Star Trek* and the *Simpsons*. It wasn't until I started school and spoke a little bit of English that I realized *Star Trek* was a fictional show.

We went to big supermarkets that had everything anyone could ever dream of. We learned silly tricks like denting a can of soup and getting it for half the price, or breaking the wrapper off of chocolate bars and achieving the same result. We didn't know any better, especially us younger ones. We later learned that this was just as bad as stealing, even though we did pay for the products at half price. We walked around the alleys of the neighborhood picking up aluminum tips off of cans and stuffing them into empty milk jugs thinking that they would make us rich.

Every day was an exciting adventure and America was everything I had hoped for. The family hosting us was a great blessing, and they had everything to do with the way we perceived our new country. They constantly encouraged us to learn English and share the blessing bestowed on America. It was so much more than anything we had ever fathomed.

We frequently ate at restaurants and were introduced to food that we had never eaten or heard of before. My favorites were Chicago hot dogs and pizza. We were getting spoiled already. I couldn't wait to tell Mom, Dad, and my sisters about pizza.

Meanwhile, they ate hot dogs with ketchup and Wonder Bread, a meal I later came to enjoy.

After about a month we settled into an apartment just in time for Christmas. *"Unchiu"* John, Mom's brother and my favorite uncle, who had already been living in Chicago for a decade, decided to give us the most unforgettable Christmas surprise. He dressed up as Santa Claus and showed up at our door with three huge white plastic bags full of toys. That night our apartment burst with excitement as we eagerly emptied out the plastic bags. My brothers and I quarreled playfully over who got what. We were desperate to see what surprises were in store for us. One of us wanted the stuffed teddy bear, another the little plastic police car with sirens, and another the basketball. Eventually we each found something to make us happy. What a special Christmas this was for our family!

In Romania we didn't have toys like these. Our toys were made of red clay from a nearby mountain that the villagers often used to paint their homes. Other toys typical in our village were sticks, sling-shots, and other hand-made artifacts.

In addition there was a sculptor in our village who made wooden guns for the kids who made good grades. It was the only toy I remember having, as well as a little magnet, which I lost and grieved over for many days. The family soccer ball was set aside for Saturday and Sunday only. Toys or not, we still had fun. Most of our entertainment came from having animals and playing hide and seek. Now, we were surrounded by more toys than we had ever seen. What an incredible feeling! I wanted to get my hands on a toy that I could possess forever. What a marvelous night for a young boy!

In the midst of all the excitement I walked over to where Uncle John was chatting with Mom and I reached up to him and said, "Thank you, Unchiu, Thank you." "For nothing, just enjoy it," he replied. "One day you'll grow up… you'll have your turn, and hopefully you can do the same." As I walked away looking for the police car I overheard him saying to Mom and Dad, "Can you believe it? This same time last year you were in the midst of a revolution and that tyrant, Ceausescu was being executed. Now you're here beginning a new life." "…by the grace of God," Dad replied.

"Sandu, you have an army here," he said to Dad. "Embrace the culture and open your horizon. There's so much you can accomplish here with all your children." Dad was reluctant to respond. Both Dad and Mom had heard stories of Romanians who had moved to America and their children grew up and went off the deep end. No doubt it was a culture shock compared to the simplicity of our village and Dad was a bit overwhelmed and frightened. Mom, on the other hand, was more of a forward-thinker, like Uncle John, knowing the opportunities were vast. But she was also aware of the responsibility. The most important thing to both Mom and Dad was faith. They knew faith would be the key to keeping us grounded and united.

Integrating into Chicago life was so much more different and difficult than we had anticipated. We had come from a remote Romanian village where there was no phone, no running water, no electricity, and no supermarkets. All that we had in our village was a tiny elementary school, a church, a cemetery, and a discotheque. Chicago, the third largest city in the United States, had a large Romanian community, but they were very indifferent toward us. We would wait around for hours to catch a ride anywhere. It was burdensome for Mom and Dad to ask anyone for help because everyone had such busy schedules. Plus, there were just so many of us. Hospital visits took forever and circling Chicago to register for welfare and other social programs offered was a nightmare. We either had to walk or wait for three different cars for all of us to cram into. Even as a little kid, I wondered how we would finally evolve into being like the Romanian-Americans that I met at church. There was a huge gap between us and them which was obvious and hard to ignore. They dressed nicer, ate better, and drove nice cars.

We soon realized that life in America was extremely fast-paced and it seemed that everyone lived very busy lives compared to our simple ones. We were just trying to get by and had to rely on the next good Samaritan to give us a ride or help us out with food.

We lived in a two-bedroom apartment in a building owned by a member of the Romanian church. At night there was constant movement in our apartment because there were thirteen of us living within such a small space. The guy who lived below us was a hothead. He would constantly come to our door and complain about the noise. He used the end of his broomstick to beat his ceiling any time we walked around. We couldn't help it. The floor was old and any time someone walked on it, you could hear the creaking noises of the hardwood. He furiously complained and made threats every night to the point that it almost drove us out of there. The guy was a lunatic. We later learned that he went to jail for aggravated assault.

We felt trapped in some kind of prison. We couldn't really go outside, because it was cold and very dangerous. In the early '90's Chicago was experiencing its highest rate of homicides since the '70's. In fact it was considered the murder capital of the country. So the only time we went out was on Sundays when a distant relative would come and load us all up in his white, windowless, work van to take us to church.

Church services were long and boring like most Romanian Pentecostal services are. The men sit on one side of the church and the women on the other. There is almost one hour of corporate prayer followed by songs and a long sermon. But at least it gave us a chance to meet new people and interact with other kids.

In the spring of 1991 we started school. We had to walk a couple of miles to get there. None of us spoke English so we were all in the ESL program at the beginning. It helped us learn the language faster. The school was immense and the students were of many different nationalities.

After several weeks I made a friend. His name was Hakim and he was from Iraq. We didn't understand each other very well, but during recess we played catch in the school yard. We also walked to school and back together. One day he was not at school and I walked home by myself. I was followed by a small gang of Cambodian kids who lived in my neighborhood. They followed me closer and closer until I finally entered a small supermarket to take refuge. I knew the Puerto Rican girl working there because she was friends with our neighbor. "Some kids are following me," I whispered across the counter. She walked out with me and looked around, but didn't see them anywhere. "Don't worry Sam, they're just punks. If you see them again run home and get your friends." As soon as I got past Kedzie Street I noticed them waiting for me. They chased after me like hungry vultures. Then they jumped me and brought me down to the ground, kicking me over and over until I was almost unconscious. They ran off, leaving me bruised and sore. I was all wet and muddy from lying in a puddle of dirty water. I was afraid to finish my walk home, so I went back into the supermarket and called Cornel, my older brother, to come get me. He was my fearless and courageous brother. He always looked out for me. "I'm going to teach you to defend yourself and these devils will never pick on you again," he told me. But my parents reprimanded me for walking home alone. "That's what happens when you don't stay with your brothers," said Dad gallingly. It was a hard lesson to learn. I never could figure out why they beat me up. I had never done anything to them or even said anything to them. That day I learned to walk in groups and to stay away from bullies.

School ended and the weather was gradually getting nicer. Chicago winters were pretty harsh, but summers were spectacular. There were always a lot of outdoor activities. Many times the church organized huge park picnics where we would play soccer, volleyball, and barbecue all day. Once we went to Silver Lake, which was about an hour away from Chicago. I had just turned nine and had no concept of what it felt like to be in a lake. I'd been in knee-deep water before in a mud-filled creek outside our village, and once when I fell into the freezing pond where I lost my shoe. But this was my first time swimming in water that covered my whole body. The experience was indescribably fun and we repeated it every time we had the chance.

Every new concept that we were introduced to or that we had to adapt to was somewhat intriguing. I began to like Chicago and I was coming to appreciate and embrace this new lifestyle.

For weeks at a time we would go to a farm in Indiana. It was owned by the family who had helped us immigrate to America. They had acres of watermelons that we helped cultivate and harvest. It was a pleasant experience, and a small taste of our former life. It was also refreshing to get away from the busy city life of Chicago.

When summer was over, we changed schools because we moved to a different neighborhood. My uncle was establishing the European American Association, to help immigrants deal with the transition to the United States. After school we would travel around the neighborhood with him to pick up trash and remove graffiti from the walls and the bridges. My uncle loved Chicago and always had a great devotion to serve, much like my mother. We planted community gardens, had walk-a-thons, and did all that we could to enhance our newfound community. It was enough to keep us busy and it helped us integrate into the culture.

Ghetto Days

Chicago was a great place to begin our new lives. It was a bit overwhelming at first, but a vibrant city with many cultures nonetheless. Two years later, just as we were beginning to acclimate to the winds of Chicago, Mom and Dad took a trip to Tennessee and loved it.

Within a short time we made our next big change and moved to Knoxville, Tennessee. There were so many of us and neither one of my parents had a job. Mom had to be home to care for the house and the younger ones, and Dad had a serious back injury preventing him from doing anything that required physical labor. So we moved into the poor and dangerous government housing projects because that was what we could afford.

Christenberry Heights would be our neighborhood for the next six years. Eventually, through the help of Habitat for Humanity, we were able to get a low-cost home. It was our first real home in America and to this day, my parents still live in it. However,

Christenberry Heights was a new chapter in our American life. It was much different than Chicago. It was so different that at times it seemed like a totally different country within the same country. But it was more affordable, and since we were struggling to make ends meet, it was our only option.

After leaving a two bedroom high-rise apartment in the gang infested, inner city area of multicultural Chicago, we were eager to move to a rural area, in a sense, more like Romania; slower-paced, more mountainous, and mellower. When we arrived in Tennessee, we absolutely loved it. It truly was a beautiful state. My parents foresaw Tennessee as the place where our family would blossom and take advantage of the many opportunities offered by this great country. But it wasn't to be so. Instead we woke up to the grim reality that unlike the melting pot of Chicago, many of the locals were spiteful and hostile toward immigrants, especially those living in the cities' ghettoes. I began to wonder if all immigrants had to go through this. We left the hardships of Romania for a better life, but our struggle in Knoxville was nothing compared to the adjustments we had to make in Chicago. I had many questions, "Was it this difficult for everyone? Wasn't America a country of immigrants anyway?" The hostility was unimaginable. Making it work in America with a large family wasn't going to be easy.

In the spring Mom planted a garden around the house. She plowed the ground and planted tomatoes, peppers, green beans, and cucumbers. It wasn't the garden that she was capable of because she had limited space and the conditions weren't great, but she did what she could with what she had. As the tomatoes grew, and just weeks before they were ripe and good to eat, kids from the neighborhood would take them and smash them against our house. This made Mom very sad, and it made me very angry. All the hard work that she had put into that garden and then some malicious scoundrels would get a kick out of destroying it. We were helpless. The thing that irritated me the most was that they did it deliberately in front of us, trying to provoke us, knowing that as immigrants we were not looking for trouble.

One day I'd had enough. I got so mad that I took a tomato and threw it back. Suddenly a gang of kids chased after me. I ran back into the house and shut the door. I looked out the window and they were jumping on the used Subaru that we had just bought. What were we to do? If we called the police things would only escalate and that wasn't what we wanted.

The next day, while waiting for the school bus, some of the kids who jumped on our car were trying to instigate a fight. "There's the Romanians," said one as he came charging toward me, shoving me and tossing my books to the ground. "Look dude, I don't wanna fight," I said reaching for my books. He then swung at Danny's head, but Danny managed to dodge the punches. Another tackled him from the back. Suddenly there were a group of them, blacks and whites, kicking and punching Danny. I jumped in to help. I got a few punches in before I was brought to the ground with him. As I was getting kicked all I could think about was my homework and getting on the bus. But where was the bus? "Get up you immigrant pussy, get up and fight," said one of them, as he kicked my books and trampled on my homework papers. I couldn't... I was angry, but we were helpless. We just couldn't win... we would never win. There was no one to defend us. Emmanuel wasn't there and even if he was, we would be outnumbered by the crowd of bullies. I was disheartened. I knew the day would come when I could retaliate, but I made a promise to myself that instead, I would find a way to stop the malice against helpless people.

The kids at school were nicer. I asked my teacher why the neighborhood kids were so hateful. He looked at me and said, "You guys live in the ghetto, that's why." Ever since that day, I did everything I could to help my parents and the family escape the ghetto.

There was a Mexican-American family of five in the neighborhood with whom we eventually became friends. They were all born in the United States. We were able to bond with them because they were different than the other kids. Often at night, Emmanuel, Danny and I, along with two of the boys, Larry and Raymond, would play cops and robbers. I loved playing the cop. At school I joined the D.A.R.E program and spoke to Officer Bowman about what went on in my neighborhood. He just marveled and listened.

I remember waking up to loud gunshots one night. I jumped on the floor fearing bullets would penetrate my window. In the morning I went outside and the garbage dumpsters were still smoking from being set on fire all night long. This was a daily routine in the projects. I walked behind my house, and there were a few blades, big bullets, and empty shells next to the stairs. I lifted a large piece of blood-sprinkled plywood, and underneath it were small baggies of marijuana, crack rocks, and more bullets. I was gripped by fear so I left everything as it was. Every evening a group of thugs would be there gambling, smoking pot, and drinking alcohol. For fear of retaliation I left everything untouched. But I told Officer Bowman and to my surprise, he said he would do some investigating. I don't think he ever did.

Furthermore, there was always the constant fear of having our house broken into, of getting picked on, and being threatened by other kids. Hearing random gunshots became commonplace. Seeing drug dealers at every corner made me question what this new life was all about. Many kids I grew up with, including one of the bullies from the bus stop, were murdered while in their teens. There were gun fights and hatred all around us. I never expected to encounter this in Tennessee. Another Romanian family that lived in another ghetto in Knoxville had their house broken into and were robbed of everything valuable. Two of the boys in the family were even stabbed, one nearly died.

Oh, how I missed Chicago! I definitely missed Romania and I missed speaking my own language with kids that would not make fun of me because I had an accent. These were some of my most difficult childhood memories.

The Spirit of Christmas

The highlights of living in Tennessee, however, were the holidays. Churches, the United Way, the Salvation Army and other charities would come to the neighborhood and assess everyone's needs. In the "ghetto" there was always a need and there was always an opportunity for people to give.

I remember our first Christmas in Knoxville. It was December 1993, and we were in for a grand surprise. By now we were connected with a few of the local churches who were aware of our condition and offered to give us some assistance. There was one particular church who told us to make a wish list of everything we wanted for Christmas. At that time I didn't know what a wish list was. So I asked my Mexican friend Larry.

He said, "Put anything that you've ever wanted on a piece of paper, give it to them and see what happens." All I wanted was a remote control car and a sleeping bag for when I went camping with Troop 701. Troop 701 was a Boy Scout troop I joined for a sense of belonging, and I figured it would make me tough. At that age, it was the closest thing to being a soldier or a policeman, and it was within walking distance from our house. Sometimes we would go camping in the Smoky Mountains, but I seldom enjoyed it because I was always cold and the crazy ghost stories around the camp fire at night scared me. So I would lay awake worried, cold, and scared that a bear or some freak would attack our camp-site.

Despite the fear, I kept going back again and again because it was fun.

Finally, Christmas came and a white church van pulled into our driveway. We eagerly rushed to open the door to welcome the lovely visitors and see what they had brought us. Our faces gleamed with excitement as we took turns saying "Thank you" and "God bless you" to them. Mom was still in the kitchen baking some Romanian pastries for them as small tokens of our gratitude. They paused, said "Merry Christmas," returned to the van and brought more boxes and laid them on the floor. We were overjoyed! Every little gift was so neat and beautifully embellished. The colorful wrapping papers were all different with little tags that had our names on them. Mom offered them some of the pastries she had just finished baking and invited them to get comfortable and stay a while, but they politely declined because they had more houses to visit. As soon as they were out of the door, I jumped to the gifts. I immediately grabbed the square box wrapped in mistletoe and tore the wrapping paper to see what was inside. Mom got a little upset at my lack of patience, plus she wanted us to save the colorful wrapping paper.

I couldn't believe what was inside, the most spectacular gift I had ever received, a remote control car. And this wasn't any cheap car. It was a black roadster with big rubber tires; wireless with a rechargeable battery pack. I think my brothers were a little jealous because my gift was so much more than we all expected. They didn't want to appear insensitive when they made their wish list, so they asked for strictly what they needed. But I took my friend's advice, wrote all that I wanted on my list, and got everything I asked for.

I had so much fun playing with my little car. Every day in the blistering cold I was outside exploring my new adventure. I would let it charge for four hours just so I could play with it for thirty minutes. It was a cold and bitter winter. In fact in 1993, Tennessee had one of its worst blizzards of all time and all the schools were closed for weeks. I remember making my first igloo and climbing it with the car. Like any kid, I was a little bit selfish with my new toy. I was hesitant to share it for fear that one of my brothers would accidentally break it.

One day I was on the porch and I wanted to see how far my radio signal would reach. So I maneuvered my car through my yard and across the street to my neighbors' house. Than I wanted to push it a little further to the next street. As it was crossing the street a truck came and swerved to miss it, but because the road was icy the driver slid and struck my little car, smashing the front tires. Immediately I heard a voice in my head, "See what you get for not sharing?" I was so mad at myself. I was mad at the driver. Why couldn't he stop? I felt like crying but held it in. He was a maintenance guy from the neighborhood and he felt really bad for what happened. He knew how much I loved that car because he saw me out every day playing with it. He said he would fix it for me and he did. He rigged it with some copper wires and some screws and the next day he gave it back. I thanked him kindly, but I still resented him. It just wasn't the same. It didn't turn like it should, and I didn't enjoy playing with it that much anymore.

Drifting Away

The years passed, I grew older, and things gradually got better for me and the entire family. We were finally in the house that we acquired through Habitat for Humanity. We had a sense of ownership and it felt like life in America was just beginning.

The house was in the country with a big back yard. Mom couldn't wait to get ducks and a baby goat. I wanted a little dog: Abel and Maria, the youngest children, wanted rabbits. Mom planted all sort of vegetables: cherry, peach, and fig trees; strawberries, raspberries, and Romanian grapes. The back yard was an orchard and the front looked like a botanical garden. Mom always loved flowers and she planted an assortment of flowers and roses along the house and sidewalk leading to the front door. We had our Mexican friends over, and we camped out in the back yard. Emmanuel built a tree house and Dad dug a creek bed. We kept busy and I was enjoying our new home.

However, the last years at our new home, were turbulent and short-lived. I was an adult, with a driver's license, money, and plenty of independence. High school was behind me and in spite of the many challenges and difficulties I faced both in my former neighborhood and at school, I still graduated with a 3+ grade point average. I should have done better, but I wasted too much time partying and experimenting with drugs. All of my older siblings moved away and I had little or no accountability.

It started with a joint after a football game during my junior year in high school and before I knew it, I was smoking pot on a daily basis. From pot to pills; acid, ecstasy and cocaine, it only escalated. There was something wrong with me. I knew it and my parents knew it. This wasn't what I wanted out of life. It wasn't my purpose, but as long as I remained in the same town, around the same friends, I would be helpless.

Many nights I would come home intoxicated and Mom or Dad would be awake on their knees praying for me. Mom always tried to believe the best, "Sami, you could hide anything from me, but remember, God sees everything." Dad wasn't easy to fool, "You're on drugs, look at you. You've become like one of those hoodlums' from Christenberry." Initially his tongue lashings made me rebel more, but I later realized that he was right. I knew they made a huge sacrifice bringing me to America and this was no way of conducting myself.

I had to break free... I was torn between civil service, going to real estate school, and going to college. No matter what I would choose, I desperately needed to be liberated from my present reality. Most of my siblings had already moved to Texas and I figured joining them wouldn't be such a bad idea. I didn't know what to expect, but intuitively felt very good about my decision to venture away.

part
TWO

Dreams & Desires

5

Leaving Home

For the last four years I worked several jobs. I was a paper boy selling newspaper subscriptions, a server at Shoney's, and a baker slapping dough at Papa John's. I had lived in the United States for ten bittersweet years, but I knew there was more to see, more to experience, and more to know. I was able to save enough money to buy a car from a friend of my Dad's. It was a gorgeous metallic blue Acura Legend with leather interior, a sunroof, and a disc player. It was more than I needed and Dad's friend knew it. He warned Dad that it was too nice of a car for me, but I insisted, gave him $4,500 hard-earned dollars and the car was mine. I packed it with most of my clothes and other belongings and I was ready for my next big adventure.

It was July 4 and I had just finished a good lunch with Mom, Dad, Danny, Maria, and Abel, said good-bye to all of them, before departing for the "unknown." My parents thought I was on my way to

Dallas, but instead I decided to drive over and pick up Amanda before beginning my trip to Texas.

Amanda was a friend whose grandparents lived in Columbia, South Carolina. Every Fourth of July her entire family would drive in from all over the United States to celebrate Independence Day, enjoy fireworks, and eat a delicious chicken stew dinner, which became a forty-year-old tradition in her family. This year she had asked me to join her and since I had plans to drive to Texas it would only be a short detour.

Amanda had become a good friend during my senior year in high school. She was a beautiful freshman and although I was quite a bit older we immediately connected. She was fun, mature, and very intelligent. But more than anything I was attracted to her assertiveness. To me it was an admirable quality, especially for a freshman!

I picked her up and off we went, two youngsters riding away in blissful ignorance. It was a gorgeous day for driving. The weather was perfect, and there wasn't a cloud in the sky. Though my air conditioner worked just fine, I rolled the windows down, opened the sunroof and let the fresh air flow in. I looked at Amanda and could sense her excitement. I knew this would be a memorable trip.

As soon as we were out of Knoxville and on to I 40, all traffic came to a halt. Apparently, an overturned eighteen wheeler had caused the traffic to remain at a stand still for two and a half hours. The driver had fallen asleep, crossed the median and plunged into oncoming traffic. We must have been at least a mile from the site of the accident. Nobody knew if and how many deaths there had been but it didn't look good. I said my silent prayers and tried to shift my focus to something else, but it didn't work. I couldn't help but worry about what had happened. I started having second thoughts about my trip. Maybe it wasn't a good idea after all, or maybe I should've been transparent with my parents about my secret detour...

Eventually, the mess was cleared up and by the time we arrived at the scene the ambulances were gone. All that remained was the overturned eighteen-wheeler, smoke, and a few fire trucks.

I once had a conversation with a truck driver who lived across the street from us in Christenberry Heights. "The best country to be a truck driver in is America," he said. "...it's beautiful and never boring." "Every day from coast to coast, border to border, through hills and valleys, deserts and mountains, those highways are full of travelers." I remember how beautifully and passionately he spoke of his journeys through America and what his favorite food joints were. "Every town has a unique personality and the best food is in the South." But what stuck with me the most were all the horrendous stories he told me. "At that speed, with all the weight all it takes is a small mistake and in a fraction of a second it's over."

As excited as I was to be taking my first trip, I knew that I had to be cautious and steer-clear of doing anything stupid. But I was still anxious to make up time so I foolishly raced past every car. I should have known better, but I was desperate to get to Columbia before night fall.

The interstate was three lanes with not much traffic and the mountains surrounded us on both sides. We were just about five minutes out of the traffic before a Tennessee state trooper clocked me going 82 miles per hour. My heart stopped. I knew that getting pulled over probably meant going to jail. I had to calm down before I got myself into more trouble. I had a bag of weed hidden under my belt, and if I acted too nervous he would search me. So instead of immediately stopping, I slowly pulled over, looking for a more open shoulder and giving myself more time to relax. Amanda had no idea what I was doing, but she didn't object. She just hugged her knees as tight as she could and waited without saying a word.

The officer got out of the car and came to my window. He was a tall trooper so he bent down to my window and with a low sounding voice he asked, "Your license and registration?" I already had my license out and gave it to him. I had to search in my glove compartment for my registration. "Where y'all youngins' goin'?" he inquired. "South Carolina," we both replied. He gazed thoroughly inside the car, nodded his head and walked off to his car.

My sense of unease began to disappear with every second. He seemed friendlier than I had expected, and after winking at Amanda I began to think that he was going to give us a warning and wish us farewell.

I was eighteen years old and had been driving for three years without a single ticket. "Surely he'd take my clean record into consideration," I thought.

When he returned to my car for the second time he looked at me and said, "You know that the speed limit 'round here is 65 and you was doin' 82." "Y-y-yeah," I stuttered. "I'm so sorry. I was just trying to get out of that mess." "Can't let you go son, it's the ruthless law." "But sir, please," I timidly begged. "It just wouldn't be fair.""Y'all drive safe now," he said as he walked off. I couldn't believe the old stickler showed me no mercy, but I guess it could've been worse. At least he didn't search me.

The ticket was for $250 dollars and that was a lot of money for me as I had spent all my money buying my wheels. Amanda offered to help me pay for it, but I refused. It wasn't her fault.

It was late in the afternoon and we were only half-way to our destination, so we decided to pull over at a rest area, take a bathroom break and smoke a joint. When we got back on the road we called Amanda's parents who were already in Columbia. We drove for another hour and we were just on the outskirts of Columbia when the sun began to set. Again we stopped. This time I pulled over on the side of the interstate to watch the sun rest over the Appalachian Mountains. It was a precious moment. The serenity of the sunset was spectacular. We were in a valley surrounded by shadows and just over the grand trees, the magnificent sun was lighting up the red sky. The colors of the sun were purple mingled with red and bright orange. We stayed there for about twenty minutes, enjoying the fresh air and savoring the view. We looked for deer, but there weren't any. Amanda's parents called, worried about our where-abouts. The whole family was expecting us for the ritual dinner.

When we finally arrived at the ranch I couldn't believe the amount of people assembled. Cousins, uncles, aunts, papaws and mammas from all over America, mainly the South and the Midwest, all there to enjoy the chicken stew that had been boiled, canned, and than re-boiled for forty-eight hours before being served. The crazy thing was that we ate everything except for the feathers and the intestines. It was the best chicken stew I've ever eaten.

After the stew, it was fire-works and beer until the wee hours of the night. There were at least fifty people not including kids. We all went to the back of the ranch to watch the fireworks. Within minutes Amanda and I got bored because of all the older, drunk, and uninteresting folks, so we went to her grandparents' camper which was just outside of the driveway.

There in the camper we were spending Independence Day talking and making out until we were interrupted by her stepfather who was overly-intoxicated. He stumbled to the camper and created such a scene which made both Amanda and I very uncomfortable. I decided I was not going to be able to stay the night there. I asked Amanda to come with me downtown to hang out for a while, but her mom said there were too many drunks out and it wouldn't be a good idea. I had to get out of there because after all that drama, I felt very unwelcome and out of place.

Somehow they found out we smoked pot on the way there, and that made them think I was some kind of a vagabond. So I decided to leave.

It was 2 a.m. and they didn't care. Nobody tried to stop me. Amanda gave me a big hug and told me to call her. I didn't have a map, but I've always had a good sense of direction, so I found my way downtown.

I pulled into the parking lot of a Taco Bell to roll a joint and immediately a cop pulled up next to me. Trying to avoid looking so conspicuous, I decided to roll the window down and ask for directions to I-40. The cop answered, "Have you been drinking?"

I said, "No sir, I'm headed to Dallas, and I just need the easiest way to get there." He realized I was mostly telling the truth and offered me two alternatives to get to Dallas. Then he told me to be cautious of drunk drivers. I never rolled my joint for fear of bad luck.

The shorter way was a two lane highway through the mountains of Carolina and on to Tennessee. I had already been annoyed from all that had happened at the ranch and now felt paranoid with all the police swarming like bees around downtown. I was so ready to get back on the road. With loud booms and bright fireworks lighting up the dark July night, I drove into the unknown. I had no idea what I was in for. The next four hours were going to be the most tormenting hours of my life as I drove away into mere oblivion.

Once I was out of Columbia and entered the mountains, the city lights began to fade and there were fewer cars each mile I traveled further into the mountains. The speed limit was only 50 miles per hour, but I didn't mind that at all. I didn't want to go fast anyway because there were too many curves and not enough light. I got sleepy and the winding road took me further away from any rest area or lodging place. I wanted to pull over, but I was petrified. I thought that some eccentric mountain man might come out and snatch me for some type of experiment or something. I was completely sober, but panic and paranoia took over.

Occasionally I would hear random booms that sounded more like gunshots than fire works. I was deep in the Appalachian sticks and all I wanted was some street lights or a gas station, but there were none in sight.

With my high beams on, I drove and drove as my weak heart pounded harder and faster. I prayed for a police car, but not a single car passed me. My gas was running out, so I looked for a gas station, a store, or a safe-house, but all that I saw were pine trees and beneath them pitch darkness. By now I was horribly panicked. I even rolled up my sunroof. I turned the radio on and off not knowing which was more comforting. I was exhausted and I began to freak out like never before. I began seeing things in the distance coming straight at me. My eyes locked, looking straight ahead and my mind gripped by terror.

Here I was, spending the Fourth of July driving in the middle of nowhere. It was so different than the other Fourth of Julys I remembered, when we would be downtown, at a park or our backyard, lighting up fireworks and celebrating with my family and my country the freedom of independence. I was, by all means, independent that night, but the last thing I felt was freedom. If anything happened to me my family would never know.

I wanted to call Amanda, but I figured she was probably sleeping. Plus, I didn't want her to think I was some pansy. It was five in the morning, and I knew that if I could drive for another hour the sun would be up and I could pull over and rest. Just before the sun came up, I saw the exit to I-40 with 2.5 miles to go. This changed everything. Immediately my hopes rose and I felt reinvigorated.

I pulled over at the first 7-Eleven I saw, got some gas and crashed in the passenger seat until noon. Across from the 7-Eleven was a Waffle House and it was calling my name. I ate a waffle, some hash browns, and drank a couple of cups of dark coffee. There were a bunch of truckers brunching and relaxing, taking a break from their coast to coast journeys. I overheard them talk about the eighteen wheeler accident back in Tennessee. Apparently it had been more fatal than I thought.

I told them I had been stuck in it for two hours. I also told them about my horrible night through the mountains, and they just laughed at me with odd smirks on their faces. Most truckers are a peculiar bunch. They operate in another world. I don't know how they do it.

At 12:30 p.m. on the dot I hit the road and Dallas was going to be my next stop. I drove ten hours straight, without any stops except to fill up on gas. I crossed the Mississippi River, passed straight through the plains and valleys of Arkansas, and then somehow I ended up in Louisiana where summer thunderstorms brought the rain down by the buckets. Finally I entered the flat heartland of America.

As I drove into Dallas, I noticed pick-up trucks and Tex-Mex restaurants everywhere. It was so hot and humid and much flatter than I had imagined, especially coming from Knoxville where mountains, valleys, and hilly terrain surround the city. I was somewhat disheartened.

The famous saying "Everything is big in Texas," proved to be true. Dallas was enormous compared to Knoxville, and huge shopping centers filled the city.

The sun was shining brightly and I was just glad to finally make it after twenty-four weary hours on the road. I knew very little about this city, and although I felt exhausted I was ready to explore it, but first I had to find my family.

Daniela, who was my oldest sister, was the first to move to Dallas. She left directly from Chicago after just a year in the United States. Then Cornel, the oldest brother, followed by Peter, Jenny and her husband, Ana, Emmanuel, and now me.

Initially, I didn't care so much for Dallas because I lived on the south side of the city, which didn't offer as much as the area north of downtown. Plus I didn't have a job or money and that made it difficult to go out and party like I wanted. I also missed my friends back home.

Between July and September I drove back and forth at least five times. I really had to be convinced of both the school that I was to enroll in and of the city. I also had to be ready to say good-bye to everything I had known for the last eight years.

It was a bit sad, but things rapidly changed and before I knew it, I felt right at home in the new metropolitan city. Deep inside I knew that Dallas was going to become the city I would one day be able to call home.

6

College and Work

The time had come. I was now ready to begin my new life in Dallas. It was December and I decided to start fresh and put my past behind me. The closing of one chapter meant the beginning of a new chapter. I was ready to move into what I called "a more consistent and balanced lifestyle." It sounds like a diet, but it was more than that. Until then, it had been pretty much a roller coaster ride. New in America, Chicago to Knoxville, two totally different worlds: adolescence, high school, poor, clever and insecure. I loved to party, but maintained good grades, in spite of my fast-paced yet laid-back lifestyle.

I was finally ready for some stability in my life. I moved in with my brother Peter. He was five years older than me and he lived in the alumni apartments on the campus of the school they had all graduated from. He always had a huge heart, a quality I truly admired. To this day I remain very grateful to him for his kindness in offering me a place to stay.

He charged me no rent. However he was very particular about the way he wanted things to be done. It was difficult for me to adapt to all the strange rules that he constantly tried to enforce on me. "The soap bar has to be on that side of the sink, the trash bags must be tied like this, and no television after ten o'clock." I'd walk away in frustration. "Sam, you need to lose that rebellion," he'd say, following close behind me. I didn't quite comprehend why he was being so hard on me. But I couldn't complain. At least the apartment was free, furnished, and close to the rest of the family where I would frequently escape.

As the days passed, I voluntarily quit smoking, drinking, and partying like I had, during my latter high school years and shortly thereafter. I worked on and off with my brothers doing construction and electrical work. However after three months of continuous strife, I decided I needed to find other work. They didn't have much patience with me, but I didn't hold it against them. I was going through a readjustment period where the past was calling, but the future seemed much more promising. Plus, I just wasn't cut out to be an electrician. So I moved on… I applied for a job with Delta Air Lines.

In December of 2000, I had my first interview with Delta Air Lines. I was able to secure a job in airport customer service. I also applied at the same school where my siblings attended. I was quickly accepted. I noticed many uncanny parallels between school and work.

First of all, school began on January 29, 2001, the same day my training with Delta began. The training was two weeks which was also the exact amount of time that I could miss school before losing all my credits. And there's more…

It looked as if I had to choose between one or the other, but I adamantly wanted both the school and the new job. I spoke to several people about my situation, and they all discouraged me from taking the job. They all said school was more important. I agreed, but in my heart I knew I couldn't pass up an opportunity to work and travel the world for free. This for me was a dream come true. I knew I had wanted this all my life, yet I didn't expect it to happen like this.

I presented my situation to the dean of students and he strongly discouraged me from pursuing both. He said, "one or the other, but there is absolutely no way you can do both. It's just not going to work. I've seen too many students overload themselves and end up dropping out because they couldn't carry the burden."

I knew I had to be extremely disciplined to not miss another day the rest of the semester. And what if I got sick or had a family emergency! Then I would lose everything. But I knew that if it was meant to be, I would make both situations work.

I was overwhelmed with the amount of wise counsel and good advice thrown at me. But I decided to follow my intuition and take the Delta job. Hence, I missed the first two weeks of school. It was torturous at first. I worked diligently and had no time to make friends.

I had already moved out of Peter's apartment into a dorm with Bobby. He was an international student from Finland. We hardly ever saw each other. When I did see him I had a hard time connecting with him because he seemed very reserved and quiet. He seldom spoke unless he absolutely had to. I felt totally disconnected from the rest of the students for the first month or two.

Fortunately, it didn't take me long to get to know people. It became obvious to the students and to the faculty that I was a Bistrian. We all looked so similar and by that time, six of us had already graduated from the same school.

My Soul's Delight

In my dorm room I had a little fridge that had been given me. I made myself a note which was to define my first semester at Christ for the Nations. It read "discipline brings desire." It simply referred to my reading and studying schedule. When I first arrived in Dallas I had a hard time doing either. I had absolutely no discipline and no healthy desires. My mind was still clouded from having smoked pot and popping pills for nearly two years and I've become somewhat slothful.

But I soon realized, the more I disciplined myself to do the things I didn't want to do, the hungrier I would become to conquer those demons. Soon I looked forward to mastering the many tasks before me.

Every day was the same routine: school from eight to noon, lunch for an hour, and work from 2:00 to 8:30 p.m. I didn't mind it at all though, in fact I loved it. I was so glad to be out of Knoxville and here in Dallas with a new job and a new destiny.

School was amazing, after all. It really proved to be life changing like my family had said it would. I felt a deep hunger for truth and knowledge. Every morning I would wake up at 5:30 a.m. to read, meditate, and pray.

There was so much life flowing through, it was incredible. I felt such a strong connection with the Most High and there was nothing in the world I would've traded those precious moments for. I knew then, that I was living for something greater than myself and it gave me so much satisfaction.

Every morning at eight o'clock the whole student body would gather in the main auditorium for a worship service which lasted almost an hour. This was truly a glorious experience. As I closed my eyes and joined the chorus of worshippers I could feel my soul elevating and climaxing to an ecstasy that I have yet to experience in any other way. All I could think about was the goodness of God, His unconditional love, heaven divine, and the splendid creation. It was never boring. In fact, an hour felt like a few minutes and when it ended, I was always left wanting more. Those moments were sublime and like nothing else I have ever experienced.

The airport was a good distance from campus so my long drive was nothing less than euphoria as

I listened to the music that my soul was longing to hear.

As I sang along, I felt so nurtured and complete like I was connecting to the very source of all life. It was the Most High. His presence hovered over me, entwining my spirit with His. Melted in the divine presence and lost in the moment, I would often get strange looks from other drivers as they looked at me and saw tears of joy streaming down my face. I couldn't help it, I lacked nothing and I wanted nothing, but to bathe my soul in His tangible presence. Spiritually I would soar away and before I knew it, I was at the airport. It's unexplainable...

Those moments are sporadic and delicate. I often hunger for those times again, but that was a "first love experience," I'm unsure it could ever be replicated.

Throughout that first year I maintained high expectations and the fire burnt stronger and stronger as I shared my experiences with other students, employees, and just about anybody I met. I felt so compelled to reach out to people who were hurting and offer them hope. This was my purpose, my life's calling, and it gave me great fulfillment.

The peace that I felt was so incredibly soothing to my soul and I walked in complete liberty. Many of the things that used to tempt me in the past had no power over me now. I knew that no pleasure in the world could replace what I was experiencing.

It was just so genuine, yet so fragile and easy to lose. I would constantly call my friends back in Tennessee to tell them what was happening in my life and how much joy I felt. I even invited a couple of them to come and see what I was talking about. A couple of them came at different times and saw the transforming power that I spoke of. However, a seed needs water in order to grow, and unfortunately I was so far away from them. Upon their return to Tennessee, they lost the fire, which typically happens when one is removed from the source of such a great inspiration.

I was satisfied at having exposed them to what I knew to be true, real, and life changing encounters. My hope was that somewhere down life's road they would find this once again.

Divine Occurrence

A few months later my free flight benefits with Delta were activated. What more could I ask for? Just a few months ago I was wasting away on drugs in Knoxville, letting my dreams die; now I was fortunate to be attending a great school and able to land this amazing job. I was very fortunate to have Fridays and Saturdays off, which was unusual for anyone starting out with Delta. I was also the youngest in my training class, but somehow things worked out for my good. I saw it as divine favor and I was grateful for it.

On Saturdays I would wake up early, take the first flight to Florida, and spend all day at the beach reading, relaxing, and returning home that same night. It was perfect. At that time, Delta served food on its flights and my only expense was a meal at the beach and a couple of dollars for transportation. It was also a good opportunity to get away after a week of school and work. Because it was so affordable and enjoyable, I traveled almost every weekend.

One Saturday I was in West Palm Beach waiting for the bus to take me to the beach. It was about 9:30 in the morning, and I had a book in my hand and a bag on my shoulder. I was only going to be there till the evening, but I always traveled light. As I stood there waiting for the bus, a nice older gentleman approached me and asked where I was going.

He was in his mid-fifties, tall, clean cut, well groomed, grayed hair, and seemed very intelligent. He was there waiting for his wife to pick him up. Because he was so friendly we began talking... and talking.

We talked about everything from religion to sports. He was a really nice guy and I enjoyed every bit of our conversation. He asked me what I was doing in West Palm and I told him I was just relaxing for the day. He quickly realized I worked for the airlines and told me his story. He was a retired Delta pilot and he loved to travel for free. In fact until the day he dies he plans to continue traveling gratis anywhere in the world Delta flies. I couldn't believe it! I realized how fortunate I was to work for Delta. What beauty it is, to fly the world and not have to pay a dime!

His wife finally came and they invited me to have lunch with them. I accepted the offer and went along. They took me to a Greek restaurant. It was there I fell in love with the gyro. I had a huge gyro plate, souvlaki and hummus with olive oil and fresh pita bread. I also tried the "dolmas" which were very similar to the Romanian "sarmale," only instead of grape leaves we use sour cabbage and more spices.

Over lunch they asked me about Romania, and I gave them a brief synopsis of my communist past, the current situation, and told them how badly I wanted to go visit and see the family we left behind. They were stunned when I told them my mom had twelve children. With a proud look I said, "And you'd never be able to tell. Mom looks amazing."

After the satisfying lunch, we went to their home to change into something more comfortable. They had a beautiful home with a swimming pool surrounded by palm trees and a big open sun room where we relaxed and continued our conversation. The husband treated me as if I was his son, depositing nuggets of wisdom that would mark my life forever.

"If you finish school and work hard you can do anything you want," he said. "America is a country that provides these opportunities."

"Yeah, you're right," I nodded attentively. He continued, "You just have to find something that you love doing and it will never feel like work. For almost forty years I've been flying and I can count the number of times I dreaded going to work."

I listened to him as if he was the prudent grand-father I never knew. His wife, sitting across from me, was silently gazing and affirming what he was saying with her gentle smile. They were the sweetest people I'd ever met, and I couldn't understand why they were being so nice to me. It's as if they were angels sent from heaven to bless my life that day. They had no personal interest or anything to gain from me.

They were just willing to display their love and kindness to a total stranger.

As we sat down enjoying the gorgeous afternoon, the husband got up and walked away for a minute. He returned with a 1970 issue of a *National Geographic* magazine. On the back of the magazine was a picture of him in his uniform when he was a young pilot. He was so proud to show it to me. I marveled at it and looked at him as if he was a celebrity. He looked at me and told me to keep the magazine.

As the day winded down, they asked if I wanted be dropped off at the beach or if I wanted to see the city a little. I decided to go to the city. I was content with anything and since they were so gracious, I figured it would be a good idea to spend the rest of the day with them.

We drove around the city for a while and they showed me certain historic monuments and gave me a small history of West Palm Beach. They gave me a preview of the city's rich history and the thriving cultural center it once was.

After my tour ended we stopped for ice cream. They then dropped me off at the airport. When I took my seat on the airplane I opened the magazine he gave me and inside was a $100 bill. They had to be angels, I thought. That $100 meant a lot to me. I was only making $9 an hour at Delta, which was barely enough to cover my tuition. I seldom ate at restaurants because I made so little, but somehow throughout the whole semester miracles like this randomly happened, where a $20, a $50, or sometimes more would come from where I least expected it. The point is that someone was looking out for me.

I was so grateful for all that was happening in my life, for having left home, and for the dream I was living. I had absolutely no need for anything else. This was the life chosen for me, and I was going to enjoy every moment of it.

Overwhelmed with favor and full of gratitude, I paused to think of what I would have become if I was still in that tiny village in Benesti. Would I have moved to the city in hopes for a better life or would I be plowing the fields with my father and raising livestock? I would never know.

I marveled at how a kid who grew up so poor in a communist country with five brothers and six sisters was able to live out his desires, traveling the globe.

7

My Latin Jaunt

It was Friday and I had one hour to get to the airport. I would have left school earlier, but I couldn't because I had maxed out my time with training and I couldn't even miss thirty minutes or I'd lose my credits. I grabbed my shoulder bag, shoved a pair of pants, sandals, some shorts, a couple of shirts and some underwear in it.

I sped to the airport. I was driving without a license, which had been revoked a month earlier because of a fender bender, which was clearly not my fault. But because I had no insurance, I was allegedly at fault. It happened before I moved away in Knoxville, where car insurance wasn't mandatory, like in Dallas, so I had to learn the hard way. Not wanting to pay for the other car, I got my license revoked. There's more to the story, but I still treat it like an open wound. It bothers me to talk about it because I ended up paying for everything and more.

Forgetting that I didn't have a license, I raced past every car on the highway to get to the airport. I avoided getting pulled over because the guy in front of me was driving faster, so the police stopped him. I still had to drive relatively fast to make my flight. It was just after twelve in the afternoon so traffic wasn't that heavy, but time was running out.

I drove right past the employee parking lot and into Terminal E where I dropped my car off, before running inside. It was 12:45p.m. and my flight was leaving at 1:00 p.m. One thing about pre-September 11 security was that an employee could totally bypass screening and go in through a back door directly to the gate, which I did. I got my seat at the gate and was the last passenger to board. It was an hour and a half flight to Atlanta.

I happened to be one of those lucky passengers who got the last seat on the last row close to the lavatory. The last row had no windows and I was stuck between two sumo wrestlers.

I always thought that extremely obese people should pay for two seats or should just fly first class so they wouldn't inconvenience other passengers. But since I was traveling for free, I knew I shouldn't complain. I was just glad to have made my flight.

Somehow I was able to take a short nap and relax a little. I had visions of Puerto Rico and how beautiful it was. I had never been to a Spanish speaking country before. I spent the rest of my time from there onward imagining what it was going to be like.

I was going to Puerto Rico to visit Angel, a friend of mine from school. His dorm was just down the hall from mine. He had a warm heart and a great personality so we hit it off and became good friends. He had gone to Puerto Rico a few days before me to spend spring break with his family, which he did annually, and he asked me to come. I knew nothing about Puerto Rico other than that it is part of the United States and I didn't need a passport to get there.

I arrived in Atlanta just in time and went straight to the boarding gate to get my seat. A half hour later I was soaring in the L1011, (Dinosaur) almost 40,000 feet above the ground, in first class enjoying a glass of champagne. I was only eighteen; too young to drink and too young to be enjoying all this for free, but somehow my life just seemed to be getting better with each passing day.

After a couple of glasses of champagne and some snacks, the flight attendant made an announcement about our flight time and the featured film. It was "*Proof of Life*," a film about a Marxist guerilla group who kidnaps people, mainly tourists, and ransoming them to fund their operations.

Initially these guerillas were financed by the Soviets, but after the fall of the Soviet Union they had to find other ways to fuel their operation. They turned to cocaine and kidnapping to fund their operations, continue their war with the government, and commit random terrorist acts throughout the country.

It begins with a scene of a bus full of tourists and locals driving through the mountains when suddenly a group of rebels in military uniforms stops them. They begin shooting, killing and kidnapping many of the people, including some Americans.

True, it was the featured movie, but because of naïve travelers like me, it was a bad choice. I was eighteen and this was my first trip to a Latin country. I didn't know the difference between what was taking place in Colombia and other Latin countries at that time.

By the time the movie ended we were minutes from landing and because I had been so absorbed in the movie, I never ate my lunch.

I began to think twice about staying in Puerto Rico. The more I thought about it, the more terrified I got. I was even reluctant to get off the plane.

As soon as I stepped out of the terminal I was swarmed with people asking me in broken English where I was going and if I needed a taxi. I was ready to turn around and fly back, especially after talking to Angel. He told me that his house was two and a half hours away from San Juan and that some guy was going to pick me up and take me to where his family lived. I knew very little Spanish at that time, but I decided I would use what I knew in order to familiarize myself with the people and try to reduce my anxiety. It didn't work. Nobody was interested in talking to me unless I wanted to buy something or take a taxi.

Several hours passed and the driver finally showed. He drove an old black Ford Explorer with tinted windows. He immediately noticed me because I stuck out like a sore thumb, with my timid appearance and "*gringo*" written all over me. I greeted him with an "*Hola*" and that was it. The guy didn't speak a word of English and by the look on his face he appeared somewhat irritated. I started to think that he spoke English, but didn't want to speak to me. I never saw his eyes because he had on sunglasses and he didn't seem very friendly. He wore a pinstriped suit and a black tie. I was beginning to wonder who he really was. Angel never told me whether or not he was a cab driver, a friend, or anything for that matter. He just described the car and told me where to wait.

As we were getting out of San Juan, I began to see the mountains. It was beautiful, but I was too uncomfortable to enjoy the view. We were stuck in traffic for a moment until he turned onto the right shoulder and used it as a passing lane. My heart gradually began pounding faster and faster.

I began to vividly recall clips of the movie. I couldn't distinguish between Puerto Rico and "*Proof of Life*". To me it was all the same. I didn't know much about Colombia either at that time to realize that that is where the very fabric of guerilla activity was centered. And so there I was, with my hands folded, grinding my teeth, scared and second guessing my decision to come to San Juan.

It was a jungle. Horns were blowing and people had their car radios blasting out of their speakers. Others yelled out their windows, and drove recklessly as if to escape Armageddon. I didn't know what was going to happen. I was a teenage tourist completely new to this culture. What was going on? No order, no police, no signal on my cell phone. Was I safe? The guy wasn't saying a word to me. I was terrified.

The three silent hours I spent riding through those mountains were emotionally draining, nerve racking, and bizarre.

Little did I know that I was as safe as anywhere, and that one day I would be going to a guerilla infested country where kidnappings were the norm, and every family had been affected to some degree.

It's funny how the mind can play its silly tricks, and how fear can paralyze the reasoning. For the three hours I was in that car, I was the victim of such oppression.

The Redemption

When I finally arrived at my destination I reached in my pocket and reluctantly gave the mysterious driver a $20 bill for having brought me there safely.

It was such a relief to see Angel and his family. They were the happiest, friendliest, jolliest bunch I ever met. They spoke enough English that we could communicate effectively.

I told Angel about my journey, and how nerve racking it was. He laughed, "This is America man, no worries." I blamed it on the movie and my travel inexperience.

Later that afternoon we went to a family gathering. There we feasted on plenty of good Puerto Rican food and Angel and I admired all the beautiful girls that we saw. I thought Puerto Rican women were the goddesses of this world. I noticed one that kept looking my way. She captivated me with her alluring eyes and her infectious smile. I timidly looked back and away. We were in a gazebo-type building and she was directly across from me. She had beautiful wavy dark hair and big gorgeous brown eyes. I told Angel about her, but I couldn't make a move. Her beauty had me paralyzed. Eventually we left and all that remained was a vivid picture of her in my mind. I thought a lot of her and hoped to one day meet and marry a girl just like her.

We left there only to go to another reunion at Angel's aunt's house. The goddesses had vanished, but I still looked forward to a good time, even though I was exhausted. In fact I was ready for bed, but for Angel and his family the night was just beginning. Puerto Ricans are lively people and their capacity to stay up all night, talk, laugh, and enjoy each other was much greater than mine.

We had wine, we listened to music, and we talked until my eyelids couldn't stay open anymore. It was well after midnight and I though the party was ending. I tried hard to stay awake and I knew it would be ill-mannered to fall asleep, but I just couldn't fight it any longer. I finally passed out on the couch next to Angel.

At five in the morning I awakened to Angel's smiling face. "You OK bro'? Let's go home." I smiled back and said nothing.

The next morning I woke up to the smell of "*café con leche*" and Puerto Rican pastries. It was only 11:00a.m. and they were ready for another day after just a few hours of sleep. I couldn't believe it.

Shortly after breakfast we grabbed our swimming trunks and headed for the beach. It was a gorgeous day and the water was crystal clear. The beach front was a blanket of white sand, with tall, slender palm trees and full of people, some swimming or lying out in the sun, others pushing carts of snow cones and other goodies, trying to make a buck.

After being in the sun and enjoying the sea all day, I was dehydrated and hungry. Angel and I walked over to a palm-branch-covered-shack where they served food and drinks. I passed on some Bacardi and asked for a bottle of water. Angel quickly stopped me. "Wait, you gotta try something else."

Right outside the shack was a young kid with a basket of big, green coconuts and a machete. Angel asked the kid for two. He took the machete and violently chopped the top of the coconut open. He gave us a couple of straws and smiled. I never had coconut water before. It wasn't that cold, but it tasted good and it was healthy and refreshing.

We then sat down and ate "*arroz con pollo*." I wanted some seafood because it was everywhere, but rice and chicken was supposedly the typical dish in Puerto Rico. It was seasoned to perfection and for $3 I couldn't ask for anything more.

That evening we went out into the town square to hang out. I realized what a big role music played in Puerto Rican culture. It was everywhere and it was loud. As we strolled around listening to guitars and drums, I noticed all the beautiful Puerto Rican architecture. It strongly reflected the island's rich Spanish heritage. Most of the town square and the vicinity had straight and narrow streets with pastel colored houses and big wooden balconies. The entrance to most houses was usually through a big heavy wooden door that opened up to an inner courtyard much like southern Spain. That was where family and friends would stay up late talking and enjoying community life. In a way it reminded me of late summer nights in Romania where neighbors and friends would gather in their courtyards for hours to gossip, tell tales, or spend quality time together. There was an appealing element to the simplicity of such a lifestyle, and the bond the people within a small town enjoyed. The difference being that in Puerto Rico they enjoyed the luxury of the pleasant weather year round.

The next day I got on a bus to go back to the airport. This was nothing like my trip from San Juan. My anxiety had disappeared and I was able to enjoy the trip back, chatting with the locals and enjoying the beautiful panorama of the island's beauty.

I loved the mountains and many of the exotic flowers that I saw. I noticed what a colorful country it was, and I felt like the two and a half days just weren't enough. I knew that I had left a part of me in Puerto Rico and my soul was beginning to cling to the Latin culture.

It was Sunday and typically during March, destinations such as Puerto Rico are populated by spring breakers, making it difficult for standby travelers.

The flights were completely full and I spent all afternoon trying to catch a flight back home. I had both school and work the next day and there was no way I could miss either. After the last Delta flight departed, the gate agent advised me to buy a discount fare on TWA to Miami. It was a late flight and it had plenty of seats. I would arrive in Miami with just enough time to make a connection to Atlanta and on to Dallas.

I had a coach seat, but the flight attendant was so sweet, she moved me to first class. I slept the whole way back. In Miami all the flights to Atlanta were full so I had to take a taxi to Fort Lauderdale, which was a good idea, because they had a direct flight to Dallas. A few hours later I was back in Dallas and ready for school and work.

It felt as if I had been gone forever because of all that I had encountered during my short visit. The Latin culture had strongly captured my imagination and sparked within me an insatiable interest that would continue to grow.

8

Homecoming

It was July 9, 2001, and I had finished my first semester without missing a single day. The time to visit my home country had finally arrived and I was as anxious and excited as I'd ever been.

At 4:30 a.m. I was wide awake and restless. I'd been up all night haunted by dreams of Romania. I had no idea what it would be like now, but ever since I left in 1990 as a young boy, I felt a desperate longing to return to my country. I yearned to visit my village, see my house, family, schoolmates and to see if they still remembered me, or even if I would remember them and everything else I left behind.

I knew things wouldn't be the same. Times had changed and people also change. Both of my grandmothers had passed away during our time in America and only my parents, my sister Daniela, and my two brothers Cornel and Peter returned to visit. Emilia and her husband had three boys now and they were still living in the same house in Ineu where I visited them when I was seven. Monica, our beloved horse, had died after a long and faithful life to her second owner. But no matter what I would encounter, I was as excited as ever to make the trip.

On the way to the airport I stopped at an ATM to get some cash. Every paycheck was just enough for my tuition, sometimes less, but with school out I managed to save $270. I figured it would be sufficient for my travels within Romania, including souvenirs and charity.

Mom had gotten us accustomed to something very valuable she had learned from her mother. Every time she visited a poor family she felt compelled to give something. She believed it was our duty to help anyone less fortunate. It didn't matter whether it was food, clothing, or money. We were taught to share our blessings with those in need, as others shared with us when we were in need. I knew I would encounter plenty of need in Romania. Plus, it was almost an obligation for anyone traveling from America to bring something to those back home.

Ten years had flown by, and I couldn't believe I was finally on my way. The anticipation grew with every passing moment. I flew into Paris, but I was only there a few hours before flying to Budapest.

It was early July. Schools were out and the buzz of summer tourists and travelers was evident. I arrived in Budapest at approximately four in the afternoon. Waiting in line for passport control I heard a couple speaking Romanian and I noticed people waiting with name signs for passengers coming off the plane outside the sliding doors. Among the names were many Romanian names. This made me feel closer to home already. I walked outside and many cars had Romanian license plates. I was so ready for my homecoming!

I looked around the Ferihegy International Airport and realized how beautiful and modern it was. I wondered if Romania would look the same. I was soon going to find out, but first I had to take a shuttle to the central bus station where I would find someone to take me to Romania. It cost me $10 to get to the station and I was down to $260. I took my stash of cash and put it in the inside pocket of my shorts as a precaution.

We drove into the bus station, where I noticed many minibuses going to Cluj-Napoca, Brasov, Sibiu, and just about any other major city of Transylvania. As I got off the shuttle, I was immediately approached by two men in black suits wanting to help me with my suitcase. I politely refused their assistance, because I was only carrying one bag. I thought it odd for a minute, but then decided it was just great European hospitality.

I was all smiles, eyes wide open, breathing in the fresh air of Eastern Europe. I had changed into my summer clothes at the airport because I wanted to make a good impression coming from America. I had a jean jacket now, but it was too hot for a jean jacket. I put on a pair of white shorts that I had purchased just before my trip, a blue polo shirt, and white Adidas shoes.

I felt a bit lost and out of place, but I was enjoying the moment too much to worry about the potential dangers a young inexperienced tourist may face in a crowded bus station.

Thorn in My Side

There was no official office or counter where one could buy a ticket. It was actually pretty confusing and chaotic with people standing around looking tired and perplexed. Basically, I needed to find the right driver, give him $20, and hop on the bus. I could not distinguish between the drivers and the passengers so I just wandered around asking. Within minutes I was approached again, this time by four men wearing black suits and dark sunglasses.

They asked me in English for my passport, where I was traveling to, and if I was carrying any weapons or foreign currency. I timidly and surprisingly answered, "No, why?" They said they were with the Hungarian government and that they were randomly checking tourists for fake money and weapons. I tried to walk away, but they cornered me. "If you don't cooperate you will spend your vacation in a dirty Hungarian prison," one threatened. I showed them my passport, my empty wallet and told them, "I only use credit cards."

There were people all around, but everyone was minding his own business. I was trapped in the middle of the four intimidating men, but I tried to remain calm. I figured that they would eventually give up after going through my wallet and my suitcase. Then, one of them began to pat me down. I objected by pushing back, but he grabbed my arm and flashed an anonymous badge in front of my eyes and said, "You're one step closer to going your way or to prison. You decide."

He patted me down and felt the wad of money which I had on the inside pocket of my shorts. "Aha, so you are carrying foreign currency?" "Yes," I said in a vacillating tone, "but it's not for me." "It's OK," he said. "We just have to verify its authenticity and you will be on your way."

I looked closely as he went through every twenty knowing that something was wrong with this picture. These were professional thieves, preying on naïve tourists, but I didn't know what to do. He then passed the money around to the other three, causing me to lose my focus. He looked at me, gave me the money and told me I was cleared to go.

As soon as I got the stash back, I counted it and realized I was $100 short. The thieves vanished. I looked around, but they were nowhere in sight. I was so disgusted, but I didn't know what to do. The minute they approached me I felt uneasy, but I had no other alternative. I hoped that they wouldn't rob me and leave me penniless. I prayed that this would be the only such experience, and hopefully this would be all I would lose along the way.

I was skeptical of everyone now. I walked over to an old woman wearing a dark scarf on her head and chewing sunflower seeds. I asked her where I could buy a ticket to Romania and she shrugged her shoulders, shook her head, and mumbled something. Just as I walked away I noticed a beautiful girl loading her bag onto a yellow bus that had a Cluj license plate. She was nice enough to point me to the right person. "That guy... not very friendly," she said. He was wearing flip flops, very short shorts and a dirty under shirt. I walked over to him and he rudely asked for my passport and $20 as he blew cigarette smoke in my face and grabbed my bag.

I was afraid to say anything else to him because I thought he may somehow be connected to the guys that robbed me. I was in a state of complete paranoia. Just minutes earlier my heart had been pounding with the excitement of being one step closer to my country and my people, and now it was throbbing with fear and anxiety.

After waiting for an hour in that treacherous station and driving around Budapest picking up other passengers for another hour, we were finally on our way. The sun was already setting and I knew little about my transition into Romania. I was exhausted, but fear kept me awake. I still had a seven hour ride in the crowded and smelly minibus before I would arrive in Cluj-Napoca, which was located in the very heart of Transylvania.

Since it was summer and this was a weekend, the border was full of cars, both coming and going. Romania had not yet joined the European Union so it was difficult for Romanians to leave Romania, but I never figured out why it took so long to enter Romania. We had to wait for four-exhaustive-hours in a long line, while border control officers went through every bag. Finally we crossed into Romania. I had my disk player in my bag and one of the border agents asked me if I would give it to him. I nearly coughed it up because I was still frightened from the incident at the bus station. But as I turned to give him my passport I offered to sell it to him. Once he realized I had a blue United States Passport, he shied away.

The communist spirit still lingered... After crossing the border, the driver of the minibus went insane at the wheel. He was driving like a madman, smoking every minute and drinking who knew what. The music was loud and we were on a two lane highway through mountains that I was dying to see, but it was too dark. He passed cars, buses, and big rigs with very little space in between. I knew that sooner or later we would be involved in a head on collision if he continued driving so recklessly.

I was as annoyed as I'd ever been by everything I had experienced: getting robbed, waiting at the border several hours, and riding with this daredevil at breakneck speed at 3:00 in the morning through the winding roads of the steep Transylvanian Alps. I never imagined this trip would be so traumatic. I was off to a crappy start. I'd waited too long to have this kind of an experience. At this point I was just hoping that my stay in Romania would be pleasant enough to make up for this mess.

Latent Wonder

It was five in the morning when we descended into the valley where the city of Cluj-Napoca silently slept. By now I had been awake for more than forty-eight hours and I was emotionally and physically drained. First I went to my brother's house, but he wasn't at home. Apparently he was at a youth camp deep in the mountains away from the city. I wanted to stay in Cluj, but I didn't know anyone and it was too early in the morning to make any other contacts.

For a $1.50 I took a taxi to the train station and I was on the next train to Brasov. The train wasn't new and modern like I was expecting. In fact it was the same old train that we had taken to Bucharest ten years earlier. It was loud and dirty and the windows were open and the bathrooms smelled horrible.

Nevertheless, it felt like the most amazing train ride of my life. I stood up for five uninterrupted hours in awe, breathing and absorbing the beauty of the country I had left behind. There's nothing more beautiful than driving through Transylvania in the summer. The sun was slowly rising over the land and the blend of colors was spectacular. There was a quiet peace on the plains and the clean air felt incredible. The plains gradually morphed into rolling hills, and the sounds of birds singing was heard even through the rattling noises of the train. I felt as if I was in a scene of a fairy tale.

What a huge contrast from the nightmare I had just experienced. It was the paradise I'd been longing for. As far as my eyes could see there were fields of golden agriculture, both grain and sunflowers. As we got closer to the mountains, the air became cooler and the smell became fresher. Flowers of blue, red, and white were still blooming along the mountain-sides. Eventually the mountains became the backdrop of tiny villages with small brick houses and orange ceramic roofs. It was truly a sight to live for.

There were villagers working the fields, planting crops, and collecting ripe harvests. I espied a young boy with a herd of sheep on one mountain, and a few meters further on a flat plain, an old man with his horse carrying a cart full of hay. This all brought back memories of when I was a kid in our tiny village working with the family in the fields. Waves of nostalgia washed over me as the train steadily clattered along.

I felt more alive than ever. I stood up the entire time absorbed in this forgotten beauty. This was the moment I had been waiting so long for, and it had finally arrived. It's what my soul desperately yearned for, and now I was experiencing it, and it was euphoria. For years I dreamed of returning to Romania and seeing how things had changed. Communism had died just as we left and I always wondered what it would be like in the coming years.

My country has so much natural beauty to offer; from breathtaking landscapes, to the Danube River, the Black Sea, and the massive ravines, hidden valleys, and deep caves across the Carpathian Mountains. It also had so much history, standing castles, fortresses, and monasteries that have been there for hundreds of years. For so many years it had been under the iron curtain, hidden from the rest of the world. Now Romania was flourishing, and I could sense that things would continue to progress as time passed.

We passed village after village from Cluj to Brasov and they all reminded me of my home. Tiny villages, where old men, during hot summer months, sat all day on wooden benches and kids played in the dusty dirt streets, where sundown meant the animals returned from the pasture and a hard day's work was complete, where there was no running water or electricity, but the people were very much content because they had everything they needed. The only means of transportation was a horse and cart or a bicycle, and if you were lucky, an old bus that passed through the village once a day. The village market was in your own backyard and if you ever needed anything your neighbor would eagerly lend a hand. Basic? No doubt, but life was lived at its best and there was a true sense of community. The fragrance of such a lifestyle was so lovely and the element of simplicity felt so appealing. I just felt very blessed to witness all this beauty from a different perspective.

How much we, the lucky ones who were able to emigrate to America, have evolved in our life styles, our communities, and our education. Recognizing that progress is a good thing, I knew that no matter what road my life would take and regardless of what I would one day become, I would never forget my roots. I knew that I could never let myself feel superior to a peasant in one of those simple villages. The only difference between that person and me was that I had been given an opportunity and I vowed to make the best of it. Had the same opportunity been given to others, they also would certainly have made it work.

That's why I find it so troubling when certain fortunate individuals cast arrogant shadows on the underprivileged. In our family we were taught to

respect all people regardless of their economic position. Mom made it clear to us that even what we had
could vanish suddenly. There was a saying she would
often repeat. It doesn't sound as good translated,
"The ungrateful will lose his gift." Life was a gift,
the ability to work was a gift; to see, hear, speak and
move was a gift. So I knew from an early age to show
appreciation for the life I'd been given.

I am also greatly disturbed by the privileged people
in my chosen country, America, with great opportunities, rights and freedoms opting to do nothing, but
stealing oxygen and expecting the government to give
them a winning lottery ticket. This reminds me of
Dad's favorite saying, "If you don't work you don't
eat." In Romania and many other countries around
the world people would do anything to make a dollar.
For example, it riles me that people in my former
neighborhood of Christenberry in Knoxville seem
to be content living their entire lives in government
housing, collecting a welfare check every month for
doing nothing, and still showing no appreciation.
But the government has enabled them... There are so
many people in this world who would die to taste
freedom...to have the same opportunities.

Enough of my socio-economic concerns; what I
truly desired was a better life for my people and a
more promising future. Most Romanians lived very
hard lives. I wanted them to experience not only the
freedom that I'd experienced, but also the opportunities that I've had. I wanted them to have the same
hope.

I made a personal decision to visit Romania every year thereafter. I saw that the infrastructure was getting better every year and the winds were changing in my former country. I knew that one day I would return to help my people. I just didn't know when that day would come. Cornel and Daniela were already there doing what they felt called to do. Many people were beginning to visit Romania for business, pleasure, and charity. I noticed newer homes being built, and new supermarkets and shopping centers. There was more tourism, foreign investors, and mission groups. The news was that within a few years it would become part of the European Union. Of course that meant a lot of good things, but it would also mean loss of sovereignty, and to a degree, loss of identity. I figured anything would be fine as long as the Romanian people got a chance at a better life.

Ghost-Town Gypsies

During my short stay, I was able to join my family at the camp where many young people gathered annually for worship and ministry. I also briefly visited my lonely village and a few families that I knew. I went to the orphanages where I was very encouraged by so many American volunteers sacrificing their time and comfort to serve the needs of the people of Romania. I would have loved to spend the whole summer there, but work and other obligations wouldn't permit that.

Back on the old train crossing Transylvania, headed towards Budapest through the steep cliffs and massive ravines, I began dreaming of the day when I could rent a car and drive throughout the country, from the east to the west, north to the south, the beaches, the countryside, the mountains, taking pictures and tasting the beauty without being pressured by time and money.

Lost in my imagination, I was interrupted by the train's random and sudden stall, just before entering Sighisioara, the home town of Vlad Tepes, (better know as Count Dracula).

The mechanics were below unplugging, flushing, and connecting tubes and cables, beating metal on metal and yelling at each other as if someone was guilty for the train's malfunction. Concerned, flustered, and frustrated, the passengers got off the train to get some fresh air. I followed... I was looking for a "Mici" stand. Mici is a typical Romanian street dish of grilled, spiced-meat sausages eaten with bread and yellow mustard.

There was a small snack stand with warm drinks, stale pastries, and sunflower seeds, but no Mici. I walked towards the town assuming I would find a restaurant and something cold to drink. I knew I should stand by, but the street was adjacent to the train lines and only yards away.

The street was dusty and deserted with two orange phone booths, four bars, with covered outside canopies, big broken umbrellas with beer advertisements, red plastic chairs and big old wooden tables. It was summer, midday, but there were no people, no noise, and virtually no movement except for the thick dust behind me, a three-legged dog that followed at a distance, and sporadic rooster crows echoing from faraway.

I thought to myself, that either the town was haunted by Dracula, or there was a sudden Rapture. In reality Transylvania isn't what Bram Stoker's horror novel makes it out to be. But I peculiarly wondered why the town felt so abandoned, not actually spooky, just awkward... or weird. Nobody else from the train followed so I figured I should turn back toward the station, but first I was curious to see if anyone was in one of the bars.

Just as I was getting ready to enter a bar three gypsy boys came running, yelling, and jumping towards me. "Whoa," I said frightened and surprised. "Sir, please do you have some money for us?" One asked politely. "We are poor and no one cares for us," interrupted another. "Yes, we are starving," said the third sheepishly.

I knew immediately they weren't looking for trouble. They were probably eleven or twelve, judging by their stature and their vernal appearance, and they reeked of cigarettes and paint. One had no shoes, another was wearing broken sandals, and they all had holes in their pants.

Maybe they really didn't have anyone to care for them, maybe they did; either way my heart was broken and I felt compassion for them. I knew that I would buy them something or give them some money, but I figured we should first have a little fun together. "First one to tell me a poem gets a Fanta!" I said. "Me, me, me," said the trio. "OK you," I pointed to the youngest. He waited a few seconds then with a sad face said, "I don't know one." "…you then," I said to the one that looked more anxious. "Uh, uh…I don't know one either but, I can dance," he said as he started to tap his ankles, twirl around, clap his hands and make sound effects on beat with his dance. "All right, you can stop," I said with entertained laughter. "Not one of you knows a poem!" I questioned in amazement. "I do," said the cleverest of the three, as he began firing line after line in an unknown language, before the other two stopped him. "That's an old gypsy song, it's not a poem," the two said almost simultaneously.

"OK all three of you get a drink, if you sing a song," I said, as we walked into one of the lonely bars. The trio mumbled amongst themselves and after a few timed-claps joined in a powerful choir singing in their native dialect which I couldn't understand. But they sang with so much passion and soul that it sent chills up and down my spine as if it was the best ensemble I'd ever heard.

The dormant town suddenly felt alive by the loud melodies of these three gipsy kids. "I love it!" I said with genuine admiration. "I love Americans," said the older one grinning and catching his breath. "I'm not American, I'm Romanian," I responded. "You are American," said a convincing female voice behind the counter. "You know, that's right… I am," I replied. "I've lived in America two years more than I did in Romania, so that makes me more American." "What can I serve you?" She asked and before I could answer, I heard the train whistle. I gave her all I had left, 300,000 lei which, at that time, was equivalent to $20 and told her, "Get them whatever they want to eat, no cigarettes or alcohol," as I sprinted towards the train.

Back on the train I thought about them and how talented they were, and how successful they could become if someone believed and invested in them. I thought about the lady in that lonely bar. "What if she cheated them or what if she took advantage of who they were and refused to serve them?" I still wondered why that town was so silent and where everybody was on such a beautiful summer day.

I also thought about my trip. What a dynamic journey it had been and how thrilled I was to have my long-awaited dream fulfilled. I was already thinking and planning my next trip back... it would be early autumn.

It was fulfilling to finally see my home country, hear the people speak my first language, and dine with my countrymen. I kept thinking to myself what a change ten years can make. For my family and me, it was a mental change and cultural shock to go from communist Romania to capitalist America. Our horizons were broadened and we were able to see and appreciate both worlds. For Romania and its people the conversion from communism to liberation was slower, but nevertheless a significant and beneficial change.

9

September 11th

Autumn came and instead of taking another trip to Europe I was forced to face, along with all of the citizens of the world, the unforgettable day that would forever change the way we live our lives.

"I woke up to the day that changed everything, not only in America, but in the whole world," was what I scribbled in my journal on that devastating day. I was now halfway through my second semester of college and enjoying both my studies and my job with Delta. During our morning chapel the director of the school stopped everything to make the important announcement.

"Two airplanes have crashed into the World Trade Center in New York City," he solemnly said. "I'm not sure if it was an accident or if it was an attack, but as things continue to unfold I will let you know."

We were petrified. I looked at Phil, a good friend from New York, and he was bowled over looking for his cell phone. Many students were already on their cell phones, worried, perplexed, and unsure of what was happening. I thought about anyone from New York who I knew but I couldn't immediately recall anyone.

We had a moment of silence. Then, the director asked, "Please join me in a prayer for God's mercy for all those involved, the families, and the leaders of our country?"

"Classes will resume, but anyone needing to leave or get in touch with family is free to do so," he said as he released the chapel. I immediately walked outside to phone Mom, who was unavailable. It was a bright and sunny day and the temperature was just right, but the atmosphere was dark and uncertain.

There was this strange feeling in the air that I couldn't explain no matter how I tried. Unsure of what to do, I went to my next class and waited for the professor for about fifteen minutes, but he never showed. I quickly ran to Mark's apartment because we had no televisions in our dorms. Mark was a friend of the family and one of my colleagues and travel companions. I walked into his apartment without knocking. He was frozen in front of his television in his boxers with a cup of coffee in his hand.

I couldn't believe what I was seeing! We silently watched as more news followed of another airplane crashing into the Pentagon and yet another had gone down somewhere in Pennsylvania. I did not know what was happening. Was all of this real? Were we at war?

I began to feel like I was in a dream and everything was gradually disintegrating. I was so startled;

I didn't know what to do. Part of me was beginning to mourn for my beautiful country, which looked like a broken vessel in a stormy sea. Part of me was feeling like the world was coming to an end and that the America where I had hoped to realize my dreams was on the brink of an apocalypse.

I couldn't understand why this was happening. I didn't know whether this would be continuing all day or whether it would soon be happening in Dallas or in Tennessee or anywhere else for that matter.

I called Delta to find out whether or not I should go to work. They asked me to come in as usual. I remember carefully driving to work, observing everything around me, and listening attentively to the radio. As I switched from channel to channel, AM to FM, it was all about the catastrophe. I continued to listen, and then suddenly my cell phone rang. I looked to see who it was, but the number was "unknown."

"Hello, it's Sam," I answered turning the radio down. All I could hear on the other end was a roar of noises that sounded like people talking. I tried to think harder about who I might have known from New York. "...Hello, Hello," I screamed. Finally, I heard a muffled, "Alo?" "Yes, hello, who is it?" I asked frantically. "Alo, Sami, it's me," the voice answered.

"Oh my God!" It was Dad. He was returning from Romania. "Dad, where are you?" I questioned anxiously. "Alo... Sami I'm here," he said in a more composed voice. "Dad where? Where is here?" "Here at the airport. Can you come get me?"

"What airport?"

"Here in Dallas, where do you think?"

"No Dad, there's no way you can be in Dallas. Listen to me very carefully."

"Hurry Sami, I am on someone's cell phone."

"Dad, listen...There's been a major catastrophe here in the States and all the planes are grounded."

"Sami, please, I don't have time for games now. I will call one of your brothers. Now come get me. I am here in terminal...terminal 2F."

Immediately I knew he was in Paris. I said "Dad, you're in Paris, just look around you, look at the people and listen to the language they speak." Dad speaks very little English and no French so he felt totally bewildered and confused. But after twenty-seven minutes I was finally able to convince him that he was not in Dallas.

He proceeded to tell me how he had left Bucharest early in the morning and arrived in Paris. He received his boarding pass and boarded the Air France Airbus to Dallas. They left on time. He had some pasta, drank a glass of wine, and went to sleep. He later woke up as the airplane was landing. Little did he know that the plane had returned to Paris because of the attack in the United States.

He mentioned how it did feel like a short flight, but he was convinced he was in Dallas. The French doctor that loaned him the phone was kind enough to stay with him and help him get back to Romania. I was somewhat relieved after speaking to him because I at least knew his whereabouts, but I was still concerned about him finding a flight back to Bucharest.

I eventually arrived at the airport, but I was running late because I stayed a while in the car to finish speaking with Dad. The airport really put things in perspective for me. This once loud and busy airport roaring with Boeing 777s, MD11s, L1011s and almost any other aircraft you can think of, was now enveloped in an eerie silence.

Each employee was assigned to guard an aircraft. I remember being on that ramp overlooking the runway, with the sun shining its sad rays on me, witnessing the most depressing day at DFW. We couldn't do anything except wait for more news. Every plane was grounded and until late that night not a single plane was heard. At 10:45 p.m. I saw lights in the dark sky as an unmarked government aircraft was approaching. It was such a relief to see it hit the runway and taxi to the gate.

It was after midnight when I was finally given permission to go home. My God, what a day!

It was a day the world wept together and we embraced each other regardless of our cultural differences. We realized that we were all susceptible to life-threatening situations and our security was in jeopardy. We knew then that we matter to each other and we let our hearts show it.

On my way home I called Mom to see how she was handling the news and to give her the details of Dad's trip. She sounded worried, but there was always comfort in her voice. Even when all things seemed to be falling apart, Mom was hopeful. Many times I would call her just to hear her voice, because it always calmed my fears. Her assurance came from the Most High, from years of trusting, believing, and living a life of faith. She had a deep reverence for God and when she spoke it was with deep conviction and compassion.

"All the hate and all the suffering... Sami, you can never forget that someone sees all of it. I hope this will be a wake up call for anyone who values the temporal more than the eternal. In the blink of an eye, everything can vanish, including our loved ones. It should make us think twice of what we value and where our hearts are."

I interrupted her, to give her more details about the horrendous attacks, but she stopped me. "...God have mercy," she pleaded. "It could have been your Dad on one of those planes."

With heartfelt pain, her words evolved into a prayer, "May God be with the families affected by this devastation, the children who will go to sleep tonight without a father or a mother, the husband or the wife who will not have their loved one next to them. May God turn their grief into joy and give them hope."

As she prayed I began to weep. I wept quietly not knowing precisely why. I wept because my heart was tender and broken. I couldn't believe how anyone could get pleasure out of this. How demonic some-body must be to go through all that training, waste so much energy and time, to kill innocent people. It awakened me to a grave reality...

And so our great nation felt the pain that so many have been feeling for many years. We realized that day that we were just as vulnerable as any other country. The attacks produced great anger, frustration, and uncertainty. The economy was headed south and America needed divine guidance. The President promised us that the people responsible for this hell would soon hear from us.

In the days following the attacks there was an increase in American pride and patriotism. The enemy's attempt to divide us failed. It was indeed a wake up call for America. Many eager to serve and protect enlisted in the military. Others took it upon themselves to retaliate.

One such crazy guy was a man who sometimes did construction work for my brother Peter. After September 11th, he went on a shooting rampage. He was finally apprehended when he walked into a gas station with a loaded gun killing the Indian owner, mistaking him for an Arab. Other similar incidents took place sporadically throughout the country by overzealous-hate-filled nationalists.

But the majority of Americans united. They turned to our roots, our religion. For the coming weeks, even months, Americans flooded the churches looking for comfort and seeking security, searching for that "Strong Tower" that brings peace and tranquility in the midst of the storm. But it was short live… It caught most religious people off guard and the churches weren't ready. Most religious people didn't know how to respond. The spirits of the American people were broken, their hearts were fragile, and they were hungry for truth, for answers, for light. They were looking for souls with unwavering faith to lean on. But to the church's shame, the people walked away empty handed and returned to their normal lives within a short time.

The time after September 11 was perfect for a spiritual renaissance. It was an opportune time for the American church to make a significant and lasting impact on the soul of our nation and revive our destiny as a "city on a hill." By compassionately reaching out in love and attending to the needs of the hurting, there could've been a true manifestation of what I believe a real Christian ought to be, showing the world that there is no safer place to run then in the arms of a loving God. And even when all things crumble and fall there is that place of safety and peace.

My objective is not to castigate and scold an ever-frailer church. I know that many churches did reach out and that's to be admired and acknowledged, but I was saddened to see that, by and large, we missed it.

It was a giant opportunity for church leaders to help America rediscover its true faith and a chance to lead our nation to life, healing, and unity, but too many churches were interested in increasing membership.

Many people who would never step foot inside a church, decided they would give it a shot. What they encountered were the same old conventional methods.

Some lost everything and they figured that in a church they might find some comfort, peace or even a lasting relationship. Instead, many turned away disappointed, because what they needed wasn't an hour-long sermon and a few songs. What these people needed was someone to cry with, to listen to, and care for them. That's true love, that's the acme of faith.

Over the coming weeks I worried a lot. I struggled with fear and I asked God why He would allow something like this to happen. I no longer felt safe and I knew this wasn't the same America that I had encountered almost twelve years earlier. I began hearing the words of my high school teacher, who encouraged me to live the dream while there was still time. I wondered what he meant by that... I wondered if I could start a family, have children and live a happy life after all. I prayed that God would grant me that desire.

I also prayed that the world would be rid of evil and animosity and we could live in a world of peace. I prayed that those who value death more than life, that those who choose to hate, would face God's justice. I prayed that the souls of those who died would be saved and that their families would be vindicated. I prayed that our government would realize that we are helpless without God, and that all our weapons, technology, and military cannot stop the ferocious forces of darkness. This time it was a terrorist attack. Next time it could be rioting and looting in the streets, an economic disaster, an earthquake, meteor, tsunami, hurricane, etc... Only One greater than us could save us. We must humble ourselves and turn to God for our answers...

10

Alejandra

Summer was long gone, but the heat was blazing like it was still July. The agony caused by the September 11 attacks was still evident, but so was the healing and America was moving forward. My second semester was well underway and I was excited to have picked up where I left off. My hunger for knowledge and truth continued and I was convinced that nothing would sway me from my mission. However, the one thing that would dramatically change my life the most, while I was still a student, was the one thing I least anticipated.

I met Alejandra while I was waiting to have lunch one day, through Pacho, a Colombian friend, who introduced us. She was absolutely beautiful and charming. She had an infectious smile, dark thick eyebrows, long wavy hair, olive skin, broad shoulders and long legs. I said, "Hello," and "nice to meet you," and that was about it. I was determined that nothing would distract me from the deep spirituality I earnestly desired and grew in daily.

One day Mark told me he had seen this really beautiful girl at church, but I had missed her. I was off traveling somewhere. He told me her name, what she looked like, and where she was from. It never occurred to me that he was talking about the very same girl.

She wasn't easy to miss. Every guy wanted her and she knew it. One day, New York Phil (that's what we called him to distinguish him from Pittsburg Phil) invited Hannah, (Bobby's ex), Alejandra, and me to the Cheesecake Factory for dinner. During our talk at dinner I noticed a connection between Alejandra and me. I also noticed what an intelligent and bright girl she was. She spoke French, Spanish, and English. She had studied at a French school, loved to write poetry, and take pictures. Something sparked in me and I started to show an interest in her.

Throughout the course of the semester we got to know each other better. She expressed her love for poetry and photography. In class one day she asked me if I wanted to go out and take pictures, and with little hesitation I concurred.

As soon as class ended I ran to my dorm to change clothes, fix my hair, and freshen up. With butterflies in my stomach I drove to her dorm, but as soon she entered my car I relaxed. The day was morose and overcast, but all the clouds made it a perfect day for black and white pictures. She decided the best place for pictures would be downtown. So we went and took pictures, and talked, and laughed, and dreamed together until we were drenched by the rain.

We got into my car and it was too early to go back to campus, so we drove around through the rain listening to music and pretending to know the city. Almost two hours had passed, but I still wasn't ready to go back so early and neither was she. The rain gradually got stronger, the winds were roaring louder, and I figured it would be best to drive to North Park Mall. There we waited patiently for the rain to stop, but there was no indication that it would. The day's mood was as melancholic as my thoughts had been. We just lay back looking into each other's eyes, with soft romantic music playing, talking about anything that crossed our minds.

I finally mustered the courage to lean over and rest my head on her shoulder. She reached out her soft hand and began to tenderly caress my face and stroke her fingers through my hair. From then on, things intensified and we began making out passionately as two lovers who had been longing for each other for years.

With the perfect storm raging violently over us, we shared lips and sentiments of romance as the night deepened. It felt so right at the time, plus we both felt we had been depriving ourselves, so this was the moment to make up for lost time. The wonderful sensation of that day created a bond between our souls that only grew stronger.

The following day at school, I apologized for what had happened. Why did I apologize? I don't know. We both knew we enjoyed it, but we also knew that this could possibly be the beginning of something more and we decided we were going to move slowly so we could concentrate on school, God, and our calling.

A few weeks later I took her out to dinner. It was a continuation of where we left off, but this time I enjoyed it even more. By now people realized that we were dating but I never made it official.

We were always together and eventually I introduced her to my family. By-and-large having a huge family is a good thing. If you're broke, need a place to stay, need someone to talk to, or just about anything, the family is usually there for you. You go from one to another until one finally comes through for you.

However, when it comes to relationships, everyone has to give some input. It was that way in my family anyway, and it drove me crazy. As my relationship with Alejandra matured, my sisters began to object and criticize: "She's an only child and she's from a totally different culture." "Look at how she dresses... there are just too many gaps between you two." "You're always out with her. You don't even care about your family or school anymore."

I'm sure they had good intentions, but the constant criticism broke my heart and it almost ruined our relationships. They were so afraid of all the cultural differences between us that they overlooked the love that we had for one another.

That's the way my family operated and it made it very difficult for us to be together. They claimed to be concerned for my well-being and my future, and to a degree that was the truth.

For the first year it was off and on. We fought a lot. Then, we would make up and be up all night breaking school curfew and missing class.

We spent many long nights away from campus making out and talking about our interests. There was something so unique and alluring about Alejandra that I didn't see in any other girl. She had this aura about her and a sense of confidence and independence that was very appealing to me.

We became inseparable and I couldn't see myself without her. I couldn't wait to leave work just to be with her. We enjoyed each other's presence very much and it was clear that we were deeply in love.

It was tough having to choose between my family and Alejandra, my carnal passions and my spiritual passion. But deep in my heart, I knew that she meant so much to me that she was worth fighting for. I knew there was a way to make things right, I just needed to be wise and prioritize.

Eventually, as the family got to know her better, they realized she wasn't the spoiled little girl who was trying to seduce me away. Instead they realized what a sweetheart she was, and how willing she was to blend into my family and my culture. My parents loved her. In fact Mom encouraged it and often reminded me of how I always told her that I wanted to marry a Latina.

"Now that you found one, don't let anyone sway your decision. Be patient and trust in God to work it out."

Emotional Turbulence

Months passed and I finished my spring semester. I was taking another trip to Romania and I had to leave Alejandra behind for the summer. We were at the peak of our romance and I would have loved for her to come with me, but she had to stay in Dallas and finish a school project. I was headed to Chicago to meet Uncle John and from there we were going to continue together to Paris and on to Romania.

I knew it was going to be a long and lonely trip without my first true love. I looked through an album that she had made for me that contained pictures of us taken during the semester. The more I looked at the pictures, the bluer I became.

We had decided beforehand that we were going to focus on what we had to do over the summer and see each other when summer was over. Early in my trip I was already distracted and I knew that I wouldn't be able to enjoy myself without her.

I felt restless and I wanted to write her a poem. I had never written her a poem before, so I found a pen and paper and let the words flow. Some made sense, some didn't, but I kept writing until I arrived in Chicago.

As soon as we landed I called my uncle, but I couldn't get a hold of him. I waited and waited, but he never showed, so I boarded without him. I took my seat and looked outside. It was a summer afternoon, but it seemed like nighttime. Dark heavy clouds covered the Chicago skyline and it looked like a dangerous storm was brewing.

We were delayed for an hour and then we sat on the runway for another hour before we took off so I continued to write.

I knew how much Alejandra loved poetry. Just a few months earlier she gave me a poetry book by the Chilean poet, Pablo Neruda. What I had written was a far cry from Neruda, but she inspired me enough to make an attempt:

I think of her as if I am gone, but only for a moment. One last kiss, one more hug, one more, "I love you" and one more glance at her gentle smile as we glide apart like petals from a rose.

It must be just a dream I think, as I try to deny the reality that tonight I'll be without her.

Suddenly when reality hits my soul with no mercy, that moment seems forever.

I'm silent in my solitude of sadness.

The last "I love you" still echoes in the walls of my soul; the last glance of her slender body of a mermaid, her sad unsatisfied smile full of warmth replays inside my mind like a romance movie.

I wait desperately for her as if she is only running late. I wait for her infinite tender kisses which would revive my solitude, her

*love that electrifies my body and the fulfill-
ment of endless nights spent just staring at
her beauty.*

*But yet she is so far away from me. I'm lost in
a world of sadness and anguish.*

*Oh, how I long to inhale the presence of my
loved one. To see the deep stillness in her
eyes like a calm sea, to see her gleaming face
so peaceful and so vulnerable.*

*As I glance at memories of her beauty my
imagination is provoked all the more to
madness, to know that I cannot hold her in
my arms this hour.*

*My soul is full of an immense disturbance
erupting into a sad rage.*

*Then suddenly I realize, though this moment
seems forever, this forever is not eternity. I
find satisfaction in the fact that she is mine,
mine alone. I know that she is thinking of me,
clinging to me as if to never let go.*

*I think of her... I feel her love soaring on
the sad wind whispering speechless songs
of romance. As I embrace my fantasies I find
myself saturated in her love.*

*Her love is never absent from me and my love
is stronger in her absence.*

Her silent absence...

I wrote nonstop until we started to hit turbulence. By now we were a few hours into the flight and initiating our flight over the Atlantic. We were just over Cape Cod when the flight attendants began serving dinner.

Then the captain made some announcements, but I couldn't understand because it was an Air France flight and the captain's English was very poor.

The passenger next to me translated, "We are climbing to higher altitude to avoid the storms ahead."

"More storms?" I grunted. "I thought we just escaped the storms."

I've experienced scary moments in the air, but this would have to be rated as the most frightening of all. The airplane made a sudden slant as if to dodge a cloud, then abruptly plummeted into a terrifying abyss. Then it began to shake and rattle violently, causing the overhead compartments to fling open and sending the flight attendants to the floor looking for cover. Cups, plates, and eating utensils covered the floor. It was so unexpected everyone was horrified.

Just as the turbulence lessened and the flight attendants picked up and tried to reorganize, there was another drop. This time we dropped so much that I was certain we'd hit the water. The drop probably lasted seconds, but it felt like an eternity. It was slow motion and all that I heard were people yelling for their lives.

The passenger on my right grabbed my arm and the one on my left prayed out loud along with many other passengers in the airplane. I couldn't see out the window because it was too hazy and dark. I said my prayers and anticipated the Atlantic.

After all the rattling I figured the airplane wasn't going to make it to France. I sat back in my seat and thought about Alejandra and what would happen if I died. Who was she going to be with? What about the true feelings I had just expressed for her in my poem? I wanted her to have it. I wrote my name on the page and who it was for just in case. I even contemplated asking the flight attendant for a clear plastic bag to put it in.

Hours passed and the flight became smoother, but occasionally we'd hit bumps which would revitalize my tension. I couldn't go to sleep so I spent the next eight hours writing and looking at her album. I went back and forth between the album and writing until we finally arrived in Paris.

My Malev flight to Budapest was cancelled so I spent many hours in the Charles de Gaulle Airport... Trying to cope with sadness and the lack of sleep, I bought a bottle of cheap red wine. Then, joining the chorus of smokers all around me, I bought some cigarettes. This was the first time I had drunk or smoked since beginning school. It was forbidden to smoke or to drink alcohol at CFNI, which was a good thing, plus I never felt tempted to.

But there I was, in the smelly, dirty, and crowded Charles de Gaulle Airport, chain-smoking, drinking, and writing as the inspiration flowed from my melancholy soul. Initially, I thought it came from not sleeping or from the trauma in the airplane, but love was the underlying factor.

I finally made it into Cluj and this time I was able to avoid the nightmare that haunted me from my last visit. Much of my family was already there for the summer. Others lived there.

They knew Alejandra and I were still dating and the expression on my face clearly evidenced that I was very much in love and sad to be without her. I was too distracted to enjoy myself in Romania. Alejandra was the only thing on my mind... This was the first time since we'd been together that I had taken such a long and distant trip. In addition, there's something about traveling to Europe that arouses sentiments of love.

The next day I felt just as lonely so I went into the city to find a post office to mail her the poem. I hoped she would get it before I returned... I was going to be in Romania for three weeks fulfilling a prerequisite to graduate. Every student had to participate in a three-week overseas mission trip. I had an advantage because most of my family went to Romania every year for a youth camp, sponsored by my home church in Dallas and the school in Cluj.

My oldest brother Cornel founded the school in Cluj upon finishing college. Cluj was right in the center of Transylvania with at least fifteen universities. It was a beautiful city, with a great cultural scene, and a bohemian feel. I always felt that if I were ever to return to live in Romania, it would be in Cluj. Cornel was clever for choosing this city to start a Bible school. He figured there were enough young people getting a secular education and all that was missing was a school offering a spiritual education.

Every summer the school in Cluj would sponsor a youth camp where thousands of young people would come from all parts of Romania for a week of music, fun, teaching, and ministry. The camp was usually exciting and it was something fun to look forward to every year. It was usually somewhere deep in the beautiful Carpathian Mountains. During the day there were different activities organized for everyone to participate in. At night everyone gathered around a bonfire to sing, talk, and tell stories. It was a great time to bond with people and enjoy the summer. This year for me was boring; I was too distracted to have a good time. My heart wasn't in it and I only attended because it was required. I looked forward to the day when my heart would be complete and I could have Alejandra with me in Romania.

Nightmare in Helsinki

I finished camp early and I still had a few days of break left, but I decided to go back home. I called Alejandra and told her about my dramatic flight, the youth camp, and the poems I wrote her. I told her how much I missed her and how difficult it was to be without her. She expressed the same sentiments and said she couldn't wait to see me.

I had to fly to Paris again and from there continue to Dallas, but because we were in the middle of summer, the flights were completely overbooked. I knew I would be stuck in Paris for a few days, so I decided to change my plans. My old roommate, Bobby, returned to Finland and asked me to pay him a visit. I purchased a discounted fare with Finn Air and two hours later I was in Helsinki.

As I sat in the busy airport waiting for Bobby I examined all the faces that passed by. I did this routinely every time I arrived in a new country. Every face I saw was a replica of Bobby and Hannah. Within minutes Bobby pulled up in a Renault. I was expecting his old Mini Cooper that he spoke so fondly of all the time. "Bobby! So good to see you, my friend," I said as I embraced him. "You made it," he responded. "Where's the Mini?" "It's not working… are you hungry, do you want to go to the lake?" He bluntly responded. "Sure," I said as we drove off.

It was a gorgeous day and the city was full of people, tourists and locals. "Wow it's so beautiful and clean!" I said in amazement. Bobby kept quiet. He was such a cool guy, but it was always so hard to get him to talk. Even as my roommate he'd remain quiet for hours unless I would ask him something. "Everyone looks the same here," I laughed. "Yea," he laughed back.

Finally he asked a question. "So are you and Alejandra still together?" Funny he asked, I thought. Bobby was one of the guys also interested in Alejandra. "Very much together," I responded, slowly nodding my head. "I really miss her." "Yeah, I miss her too," he said innocently as we entered the park.

The park was crowded with topless men and women lying on the grass tanning and enjoying the sun. Others played games and enjoyed picnics. I felt a bit out of place, but I enjoyed it. We walked further toward the Black Lake where we met up with some friends and went swimming.

It was there in that Black Lake that I saw heaven open and my life flash before my eyes. It was much different than the airplane experience. I'm not the greatest swimmer especially when the water feels like knives cutting into my skin.

Bobby and the other crazy Vikings decided to swim across the lake to the opposite side to do some cliff jumping. It was a pretty long swim, but I decided it wasn't a good time to doubt myself as I followed them. Half-way across the lake my left leg began to cramp. Through the excruciating pain, I pushed and pushed until I reached the massive rocks.

I was exhausted, but I foolishly played it off. They were having such a blast and I didn't want to spoil their party. Before I could get a good rest, Bobby and the rest were ready to return to the other side. "Let's go," he said as he dove back into the black fiord.

I waited a while to catch my breath, rubbed my muscles and dove out as far as I could. Everyone was well ahead of me already. I swung my arms tirelessly, but to no avail. I was far away from the shore and making little progress. In my mind I was cursing Bobby, "How could he do this? Where the hell is he?" It's not a good time to blame others, I thought, as I began to go under.

I was faint. Completely depleted of all source of strength, I wanted to yell out for help or just push a little bit further, but I couldn't.

As I drooped and hyperventilated the ultimate thought came to mind, "So, this is how it's going to end." Yeah, I said my prayers, but it seemed nothing was working. Death was right there and I didn't see an escape.

I became completely submerged and, then instantly, with a small burst of energy I brought my head back to the surface of the water. My arms were useless, they were numb. I turned on my backside and began peddling my feet. I tried opening my eyes towards the sky, but it was too bright.

So with my eyes closed and only my right foot peddling just enough to keep me afloat, the melody of a song that we used to sing in morning Chapel came to me, and barely moving my lips I sang, "I need you Jesus to come to my rescue, where else can I go."

What happened next was a miracle. A young boy, or maybe an angel, who was not too far from the shore, realized I was struggling, swam towards me and grabbed my arm. He guided me to the dock where there was a flight of wooden stairs. I latched on to them until I regained some strength. I looked towards the shore trying to see Bobby and his friends, but everything seemed blurry. I could have died and they would've never noticed.

I finally walked out of the water towards the grass. My body was so weak and feeble that I just collapsed. I fell on my knees, serenading the grass with my vomit. Bobby finally found me and came to see if I was alright, but I didn't feel like talking. I nodded my head, gesturing I was okay.

After lying flat on my back with my eyes closed for a good while, I was able to get up. I had the worst imaginable migraine and I couldn't open my eyes. Everything seemed extremely bright.

Bobby felt sorry for me, but I couldn't be mad at him. He helped me get to the car where I lay on my back until we arrived at his house. They didn't fully comprehend what was going on with me. I didn't either. This had never happened before, but I was just grateful to be alive.

I was so close to death for the second time on this trip, once in the air, and now in the water. I no longer felt a canopy of protection around me. I kept asking God, "Why?" Why did he allow this? Or what was he trying to tell me? Am I missing something?

It was early afternoon, but I had no desire to do anything. I found the nearest bed and crashed. I awoke trying to remember a dream that I had just had. I couldn't remember a whole lot, except that I was in a communist country. I looked at my watch and it was after midnight. I looked outside and it was still daylight. For a minute, I thought I had lost it or that I was hallucinating. I later realized that because Finland is so far north, summers are illuminated nearly twenty-four hours by the sun. On the other hand, winters are dark except for a few hours.

Several days later it was time for me to return home. On the way to the airport I debated whether or not my trip was worthwhile. It only cost me one hundred dollars and a near death experience! I asked God to restore my passion for Him again, enlighten my vision, and make my life an instrument of hope. I was given a second chance because there was a purpose for my life. There was a destiny that I was shying away from and a vision that was becoming more and more dim.

The flights were still full, even from Helsinki to Paris. However, because I was an airline employee I was able to fly in the cockpit from Helsinki to Paris. The view from the cockpit was spectacular. It was redemption for my Chicago to Paris flight. As I sat in that cockpit gazing at the open skies, little by little, the dream I had in Helsinki came to me.

I was away from my family trapped on a faraway island. The place was identical to the backyard of our home in Benesti and I was playing my guitar and singing Spanish songs with little kids all around me. Alejandra wasn't with me, but I was OK...

11

Colombia

I was back in muggy Texas and I kept thinking about my European excursion and the meaning of the dream I had. I refrained from telling Alejandra everything, but I took advantage of every opportunity to be with her.

We spent many long, hot and humid summer nights together. The time for her to return home to Colombia was rapidly approaching so I made sure to make the best of our last days together. As an international student, Alejandra was only in school for one year. She finished a semester before me, and now it was time for her to leave.

"Stay here with me," I pleaded. "I'll finish school and we can get married and travel the world together."

But as lovely as my words sounded, she knew it was time to return home to her family. It broke my heart to see her go. Alejandra was my first true love and I couldn't fathom living without her, but I knew that if it was meant to be, the distance would augment our love.

We decided to stay in touch and let time be the deciding factor. As hard as it seemed, I knew I had to accept going separate ways if it was best for her. The time apart proved to be both sad and difficult for us. I worked a lot and was very busy with school, but I missed my Alejandra. I bought calling cards every day and I would speak to her after work. I e-mailed her and we chatted on messenger, but it wasn't enough. I needed to see her. Dallas summers are typically long and autumn seems to take forever to arrive, but this year it wasn't so. The leaves began to fall prematurely and a cool front came in earlier than usual. The dismal feeling of the season left me feeling lonely, but there was nothing I could do. It wasn't the money; I just couldn't take time off work or school.

During work we had long breaks between flights and when I wasn't talking to her, I was reading about Colombia. I read both the good and the bad, but more bad. I read about the Narcotraficante and how Colombia is the number one producer of cocaine in the world.

I read how the guerillas continue to kidnap government officials and tourists to fund their gruesome war that has lasted for more than forty years. The country has seen constant instability since the early nineteen hundreds and every president who tried to stand up to the guerillas and the drug cartel has been assassinated or kidnapped. I read about how Americans who have been kidnapped remain in the deep jungles for years and how rescue missions to save them have failed.

But the more I read the more eager I became to visit. Colombia became the "forbidden fruit" that I wanted to taste. When I told my colleagues at work they told me I was crazy. I told my family and they discouraged me. When I told Mark, he said, "Go if you wanna die."

Everyone warned me as if I was going directly into a war zone. Yes, I had to be realistic, but I couldn't let all the negative news keep me from seeing Alejandra. After all, it is a country of more than 40 million people, not an enclosed ghetto.

I happened to arrive the day a new president was elected. His name was Alvaro Uribe and his father had been killed by the guerrillas. He was a man that strongly opposed corruption and wanted to lead Colombia to a new era of freedom and tranquility.

He vowed to bring hope and decrease the violence. And because he was so tenacious in bringing both the guerillas and the drug traffickers down, they attempted to assassinate him nine times.

As I waited for the flight to board, I began a conversation with the lady sitting next to me. She was from Medellin, one of Colombia's largest cities, the home of infamous Pablo Escobar. Pablo Escobar was the most notorious drug lord to have ever lived. According to many credible sources, Escobar, before his death, was the seventh-richest man in the world. The Medellin cartel was taking in up to $30 billion annually and controlled eighty percent of the global cocaine market.

"I came to the United States in the late '80's as a refugee," she said as she crossed her legs and looked away with sorrow in her eyes. "My husband was killed by the cartel and my oldest son kidnapped by the guerillas. I sold my house and everything I had to pay for his ransom. Three weeks later, they kidnapped him again," she said reaching in her bag for a Kleenex. She was returning after nearly fifteen years to see family that she had left behind and to see if her son was still alive.

It still wasn't too late for me to cancel my reservation, but everything she told me only aroused more curiosity and passion for the visit. I listened in total astonishment as she continued. "It's changed a lot. I think this is the safest it's ever been, so try not to worry."

We talked about many other things, including the movie I had seen on my way to Puerto Rico. "Can that really happen?" I asked. She nodded her head, "It can, depends where you go." I had one more question, "Is there an island that's part of Colombia?" "Yes, San Andres," she replied. I thought about the dream I'd had... "It's not controlled by the Marxist guerillas is it?" I asked. "No, they probably vacation there. They operate deep in the mountains," she answered.

I left that conversation with plenty of information and a very helpful word, Ayudame, meaning, "Help me." She told me to yell that word as loud as I could if I found myself in a dangerous situation. I made sure that wasn't going to be a word that would slip my mind.

In spite of all the horror I heard and read I was still as excited as ever to be going to Colombia and even more excited to see Alejandra. I wasn't nervous because somehow I just knew I would be OK.

When I finally arrived in Bogota, I thanked God for having safely arrived and said a prayer for the remainder of the trip. As I sat there waiting for my flight to Cali I opened up my journal and began to write.

I left Dallas this morning at 7:30 and arrived in Atlanta just minutes before 10. I had a six hour layover so I kept busy talking to a Colombian woman about her horrible life. Now I am in Bogota and I'm a bit tired. The airport is chaotic. Outside it's dark and raining so I can't see a whole lot. I hope Cali is different... God pls, let me see Ale tonight.

I arrived in Cali, "Capital de la salsa," just before midnight. I walked down the long hallway of the terminal leading to the exit doors. It was a red carpet experience as I exited. Crowds of big smiling faces were waiting anxiously, anticipating their loved ones. In the huge and noisy crowd I noticed my lovely Alejandra. There she was with a big smile on her face, wearing a purple tank top and a pair of jeans. We embraced each other as if I had been a kidnapped victim returning from the miserable jungles.

After a few moments of kissing and caressing, we headed for her house. I was expecting a small cottage outside of the city. Instead we arrived at a beautiful white building carved on the side of a big mountain. There on the seventh floor was her parents' condo which was three times bigger than my parents' house in Tennessee. The building was designed by her father, who is an architect. On top of the building were a pool, sauna, and a hot tub. The panoramic view of the city was spectacular. I marveled at how beautiful and orderly everything was. This was far better than anything I'd imagined. Alejandra was all smiles. She was eager to take me around the city, but it was already too late.

The following morning Alejandra came to my room and cuddled with me for a while before break- fast. "It's ready," a voice hollered from the kitchen. It was Maria, their maid who came every day to cook and clean the house. "This is heaven," I told Alejandra. "Just wait," she said, "we can go to the country club, the finca in the mountains, my dad's hotel..." "Too bad I only have a few days," I said. "Oh and there's these fruits and typical foods I want you to try," she said as I was stuffing myself with *arepa con huevos*. "I'm ready," I said. "Muchas Gracias Maria," we called, and we were out the door.

We descended into the city center which was just minutes from her house. Cali is a mountainous city with houses, buildings, and shopping centers crammed close together. There were people every- where like busy ants, working and selling anything one can imagine. There were women walking around with big colorful dresses and aluminum baskets on their heads selling big green avocados the size of a cantaloupe, mangoes, lulo, papaya, and other exotic fruits that I never even knew existed. There were all sorts of produce unique in texture, color, and taste.

At every stop light there were young street kids trying to make a peso by doing various tricks to entertain the drivers before the light turned green. On the ground, were artists displaying their paintings, crafts, and leather effects.

Next to a five star restaurant or hotel would be a homeless family or a guy with a portable canister, grilling hot dogs and corn on the cob. I was surprised by the drastic differences in lifestyles between the poor and the rich throughout the city. I noticed many upscale businesses and shopping centers that I never thought I would encounter in Colombia. They were far nicer than anything I saw in Romania. It took me a while to figure out what created this huge chasm.

I later realized that Colombia is a country with a small middle class. Most people live in extreme poverty. Some study hard and have professional careers and usually do well for themselves. Yet, there are the drug traffickers who make a lot of money illegally. Most of the drug traffickers grew up in poor families. They make so much money they can afford to buy anything they want. Therefore, a demand for luxury is created.

The country clubs that we visited were evidence of this luxury and the people there were mafiosos, politicians, and businessmen alike. On the weekends people go to their chalets in the nearby mountains. As one drives into the mountains there are big and beautiful haciendas that were built by these drug lords, but many of them were now empty or up for sale.

In the '80's and '90's the Cali cartel was very powerful. Alejandra told me stories of the gangster that roamed the city and demanded respect from everyone. If anyone stood up to them, including the police, they would gun them down. So much money had come into Colombia from drugs, especially cocaine, that some of the city's economies were driven by it. Many architects, builders, and other businessmen relied heavily on the drug lords to fund projects in the city. For most of them, it was just business.

As I walked around with Alejandra I was saddened by how such a beautiful country with a year round tropical climate, great food, and good people could suffer from so much bloodshed. We found a nice café to have the true Juan Valdez experience and I asked Alejandra, "Why so much violence?" But, she didn't want to explain. "I couldn't imagine anyone close to me being murdered," I rambled on. "I mean, I knew people that were murdered when I lived in the ghetto in Tennessee and I had friends who died by overdosing on drugs or by drinking and driving, but thank God it wasn't anyone close to me."

The more I spoke, the more alienation I created. I looked straight into Alejandra's eyes trying to decipher what was on her mind. "What is it?" I asked. She was lost in another world and appeared somewhat troubled and distressed. But she answered me, "Oh, just something from the past." "What, what happened?" I curiously insisted. "Someone close to me was killed before I met you."

I was dumbfounded. She continued, "It was my favorite uncle. He was murdered in the street, in broad daylight, in front of his four children just a few years ago." She quickly jumped to the next sentence before I even had a chance to comment. "It's beautiful, but the cycle of violence doesn't seem to end." I wanted more details, but I wasn't sure she wanted me to know everything or maybe she wasn't ready to tell me.

We stopped talking for a while. I waited in silence, imagining what a world without violence would be like. *"What would it take for people to live in tranquility?"* I asked myself. You can try to educate the masses, but there will always be strife. It seemed the more people had, the more they wanted. Nothing is ever enough. If everyone would be rich or everyone would be poor, there would still be competition. There will always be envy...

Colombia was a democracy, with plenty of natural resources and wealth, yet violence superseded that of poverty stricken communist countries. I questioned which form of government was most effective or if any political system worked at all? I wasn't questioning freedom, my very faith mandates freedom. I questioned the lust for power that was behind corrupt governments, whether they are communist or capitalist.

"Eventually things will change, we can't lose hope," I muttered as we walked away.

I realized that the negative perception most people have of Colombia was justified, but there was a new, more relaxed ambiance, which Alejandra tried to express, "There is a sense of safety that we haven't experienced in a long time," she said. "The guerillas are losing strength and the drug cartel had been, for the most part, dismantled."There was clearly a lot of expectation for something better and the Colombian people were ready for a change.

The days went by so fast, and before I knew it, it was time to depart. I realized I was in love not only with a Colombian girl, but with everything she showed and offered me. I fell in love with the Colombian culture and I knew that our relationship was just beginning. Colombia was to become my "best kept secret destination" in South America and I knew I would be returning soon.

Now I was back in Bogota, in the crazy Eldorado Airport, which was extremely noisy, crowded, and disastrous. The country was on high alert. Just days before I arrived in Bogota, there was a bombing, and there were military personnel and helicopters swarming all around the city. I found my way to the Delta ticket counter where I waited and waited until the last revenue passenger showed up. I was able to get a seat in business class, but immigration and long security lines caused me to miss my flight.

I went around looking for a cozy place to rest. As I sat down absorbing the chaos and the charm, I got my journal out and started to write.

Colombia was truly a remarkable country to visit. I discovered more than I ever imagined, from friendly people to fraudulent people, great food, exotic fruits, flowers galore, spec-

tacular landscapes, and nonstop fiestas. One can encounter anything from coffee to cocaine, ajiaco to aguadiente, peasants, businessmen, goddesses, maids, narcotraficante, guerillas, and politicians. Sometimes it's hard to distinguish who's who. There's this uncanny feeling in the air, an uncertainty, that anything could happen, anytime, that would erupt into chaos. Other than that, there is a love of living life fully, of enjoying every moment. The people of Colombia know that, and though the cycle of violence continues, there is a counter struggle for peace. And the most admirable quality is their resilience. There is no surrender.

12

Graduation Surprise

Months passed and I didn't see or hear a whole lot from Alejandra. She was busy with other studies and modeling on the side. I was focused more than ever on school and making sure I finish strong.

The last two years had been two of the best years of my life and the moments spent in the main auditorium and the prayer room of CFNI impacted my life so intensely that I knew I would cherish the experiences forever. But now I had to focus on my future. I knew that learning a lot and having great sentimental experiences was just the beginning. It was now time to go out and apply some of the principles I had learned, but I wasn't sure what to do or where to start.

My brother Cornel insisted that I move to Cluj and help him with the school. I loved Cluj and all that was happening there, but I just felt like the timing wasn't right.

My job was going well, but there were rumors that many airlines were laying off employees and Delta would soon follow. It was clear that the terrorist attack of September 11 was a major blow not only to the airline industry, but to the U.S. economy as well. The airline industry had suffered most, and something had to change immediately for Delta to remain profitable. But things didn't look good. They were gradually getting worse.

Weeks passed and more rumors emerged. One was that Delta was going to downsize and eliminate the Dallas hub altogether. One day I was having lunch with Mark. "You know the rumors are true," he said. "Delta is laying off thousands and that could mean no more free flights."

"Aww, that would suck," I said, "Just as I graduate with all the time in the world to travel."

We worried about all the repercussions. It would mean at least eighty percent of the employees based at the Dallas airport would lose their jobs. I knew that everything was in God's hands, but with my job on the line I panicked like everyone else. The company was in great distress. Employees, supervisors, and managers were all waiting to see exactly what would happen.

I enjoyed two years of traveling the world for free and now all of it seemed to be ending. I prayed that things would work out for the best and I knew that worrying wasn't going to solve anything.

I gave my last buddy pass to Alejandra to fly in for my graduation and I called Mom and Dad and advised them to fly while it was still free.

Mom didn't worry. She quoted a familiar Bible verse, "Delight yourself in the Lord and he will give you the desire of your heart." Ironically it was the same verse Alejandra read to me before she left for Colombia. "God has taken good care of you. Your dream has always been to travel the world. I'm sure He will take good care of you."

Job or no job, I felt reassured and at peace with my future. The next day at work the news broke that there would be no lay offs. Yes, they would downsize DFW, but there were other alternatives they were exploring that would ensure everyone would continue to have a job.

This was sweet music to my ears. What a pleasant surprise! It was the best news I had heard all year. Actually the last time my heart exploded with so much excitement was when I found out we were going to be moving to America. It was one of those pivotal moments for me, and I waited with great anticipation to see what options would best fit my needs.

The employees were given the chance to relocate to any of the other major hubs, mainly Atlanta, or take one of the packages that Delta was offering. Employees that had more than a certain number of years with the company were able to take a special early retirement. Since I only had two years with the company and I was only twenty years old I didn't qualify for early retirement. However, I was able to take a leave of absence and retain my flight benefits. In fact I was eager to take this leave of absence with the option of returning after five years. I couldn't have asked for anything more. Delta Air Lines is known in the industry for taking good care of their employees, but this was incredible, especially when other airlines were laying people off left and right.

My family was just as astonished. What company rewards you with five years of unlimited travel benefits after just two years of service? This was unbelievable! My parents were also able to fly for free, and if I would marry, my wife would have the same benefits.

The same week I graduated, I initiated my leave of absence. The timing was perfect. Mark took the same package a month later. "She should marry you just for the benefits," he joked referring to Alejandra.

"What a blessing this turned out to be for the entire family!" I thought in amazement. Things were beginning to unfold just the way I foresaw them as a child when all I wanted to do was travel around the world. I was certainly living my dreams. What a grand opportunity! I was full of gratitude. Twenty years old with college completed and five years of free travel ahead of me, anywhere in the world. I often wondered what I would be doing if I were still in Romania. I couldn't take this for granted. I knew the Most High was looking out for me. Sure, there were other kids in the world enjoying a better life, but I was comparing it to the life I had in Benesti. Mom was lucky enough to finish fourth grade, Dad the same. Other villagers didn't even know how to read or write. For me this was enormous and I knew the key to a blessed life was a grateful heart.

I now had a pretty good idea of what my next endeavor would be. I kept thinking about the dream

I had in Helsinki, and I wanted to be a missionary in another country. After realizing how blessed and fortunate I was, I wanted to go to another country and serve and provide assistance. I had a strong desire to work with street kids. I had a friend who told me about a missionary and humanitarian organization.

It was YWAM or "Youth with a Mission," founded by Loren Cunningham in Zurich, Switzerland in the early '70's. The organization had bases throughout the world. It would be a five-month program. During this time I would learn how to live the life of a missionary by learning and applying the teaching of Jesus.

Their motto is, "to know God and to make Him known." It's that simple, but they use many different means to accomplish that mission. The organization has many outreaches in the poorest and most remote parts of the world. They go where no one would dare go, offering love, hope and a better way of life to the least cared for, the forgotten children of God. I knew this would be a great opportunity for me to give something back.

I was infatuated by everything I heard and read regarding YWAM. I was determined to try it and see where it would take me. The base that I chose was in Cartagena, a coastal city in Colombia. I told Alejandra what I decided to do, but she didn't seem too excited. I was at the point in our relationship, where I knew I should surrender our future together to God. I wanted to be with Alejandra, but I also had a purpose and destiny to grab hold of.

This was a great opportunity to work with abandoned street kids and senior citizens. I wanted to be around those living in extreme poverty and try to offer them the hope and love that I knew. I was also ready to apply everything I had learned at school and live the life of a missionary.

It felt good to hear the teachings and experience the worship, but I knew that there was work to be done. I wanted others to experience the same peace and love that I was experiencing, and what better place to go than a poverty-stricken country. I was so ecstatic about going that I never dawdled about my decision. One weekend the whole family gathered at my sister's house and I told them about temporarily moving to Colombia. They were shocked. They tried talking me out of it, but to no avail.

"Honestly I have no idea what awaits me, but I'm ready to live life on the edge, even if it means leaving my present comfort," I told them. Any fear or worry that I might've had was overruled by the zeal and love that motivated me. "It's Alejandra," said one of my sisters. "Are you going to follow her everywhere Sam? Look, maybe it's just not meant to be." I was on the hot seat getting grilled by every sibling all over again like when I first met her. "Listen guys," I said, "I don't even know if Alejandra's coming. To tell you the truth, she has plans to move to France. The decision is mine."

That following Sunday, the pastor at my local church announced that I would be departing. The six months away, including tuition, housing and food, was going to cost me $1,500 I didn't have. Almost one thousand dollars was raised for my trip by the generosity of the church members who believed in what I would be doing. That proved to be another miracle and a confirmation that I made the right decision. A week later I was off to Colombia.

part
THREE

Destiny & Devotion

13

❦

Cartagena

(The Mission Begins)

I arrived in Cartagena with a strong sense of vigor, high expectations of learning Spanish, and enthusiasm to live like a missionary. I decided beforehand that no matter what difficulties I might face, I would remain committed. I arrived there alone. Alejandra wanted to come with me, but she had a lot of uncertainty, because she felt pressured to go study cinema in France.

As soon as I got off the plane I felt like I was on vacation. Palm trees, sunshine, and water surrounded me. I got my bags and walked outside where a string of yellow taxis were lined up. Across the street were push carts serving shrimp or crab "*seviche*" and Pony Malta, (a Colombian barley drink). After a sample of the goodies I was greeted by a young couple who would take me to the base where I would be staying. Together we hopped into one of the taxis and headed for the YWAM base, twenty minutes away. I couldn't talk to anyone in the taxi because nobody spoke English, so I sat back and enjoyed the beautiful *paisajes*. Cartagena was very flat compared to Cali and Bogotá, but it was undoubtedly the most picturesque city in Colombia. The drive from the airport took us right by the beach which was filled with people. To my left was a big wall the Spanish built in 1812 and to my right the Pacific Ocean. The sun was bright and there was a calm breeze blowing through the windows of the old taxi. I thought to myself, if I ever marry Alejandra this would be the place to have our honeymoon.

We arrived at the base less than thirty minutes later. There was a message for me from Alejandra: she would be coming the following week. I rejoiced! Later, I met the staff and the students who were arriving from all over the world. Altogether we were more than thirty-five students from Canada, the United States, India, Sweden, Norway, Switzerland, Argentina, Venezuela, Peru, and Colombia. Not all of them spoke Spanish, but most spoke some English. I knew that if I wanted to learn Spanish, I had to mingle with the Latinos.

I happened to be placed in one of three houses, which housed most of the Latinos. My room was very small with four bunk beds and an old ceiling fan. Lucky for me, only one of my roommates spoke English, broken English. His name was Pradeep and he was from India. He came to Cartagena hoping to encounter a beautiful girl that he could marry and take back to India. He was a very interesting personality and we eventually became close friends. Between classes he would play Indian love songs on his guitar, charming the young girls. Then, there was José from Peru and David from Bogotá. Both of them were younger. Josué was very quiet and acted very peculiar most of the time. He would isolate himself from everyone and go off somewhere with a book in his hand. David was the youngest in the room. He was sixteen, but what a talented kid he was. He played guitar, piano, and drums. He had an amazing voice and a great sense of humor. He was a really good actor too. He would do these flawless impersonations of just about anybody. "Hi, I'm Pradeep from India," he would say before beginning to strum different chords and making identical melodies with his high-pitched voice. I would laugh hysterically as he'd play and mimic Pradeep's exact facial expressions. Then, there was Jimmy, the staff leader of our dorm, who was responsible for maintaining order and making sure the lights were out by 10:00 p.m. The reason we had to go to bed so early was because we had to get up very early. This was like a missionary boot camp, preparing us for the two months we would be on our own.

The day started at 5:00 a.m. and the first hour of every day was "quiet hour." Some spent it reading, others praying, writing, or just meditating. This time was crucial for me and in a way it reminded me of when I was in school in Dallas. At exactly five o' clock I would awake, and while it was still dark, I'd walk to the bay. Halfway through the hour I could see the gorgeous sun rising over the old city, located across this huge body of water. I'd watch as all along the bay fisherman on small boats would gather their daily supply. There was a man with a coffee thermos who would routinely pass by and I would get a ten cent *tinto* from him. This was a shot of Colombian espresso and it was just enough to wake me up.

Following our "quiet hour" we were given chores, which consisted of sweeping and mopping, cleaning the bathrooms, washing dishes, or making breakfast for everyone. Breakfast was at eight o'clock every morning and by then we had to have all our chores done. The class began promptly at 8:30. It was usually in a narrow room with three ceiling fans and no windows or occasionally in an open park or by the bay. Lunch was not something to look forward to. Well, it was better then the breakfast, which was a cup of hot chocolate and a corn tortilla. Lunch was rice with a small portion of ground beef or chicken. It seldom changed. I soon realized why we were only paying $1,500 for the entire five months. Shortly after lunch we returned to the classroom where we stayed until dinner. Between lunch and dinner we had creativity class, which was something we all looked forward to. It was during this class we had to break out of our bubble of fear and become totally transparent and comfortable with each other. We learned skits, dramas, mime, and games that we would later use to entertain the young children on the weekends and eventually for the two months when we would be on our own. There were no exceptions, everyone had to participate. The staff constantly challenged us to extend our creativity to new heights by stretching ourselves artistically and learning how to use our minds, bodies, and souls in becoming excellent at whatever we did. I picked up a guitar and began learning enough chords to sing a song or two.

One weekend we had an international event for the neighborhood. The theme was "a taste of the nations" and we had snacks, games, songs and costumes from all over the world. It was there in front of everyone that I learned what it meant to face my fears, as I sang and played my first song on the guitar. The song felt like it was never going to end, but once I finally finished, I realized it wasn't that bad. And the kind applause, the energy, and the cheers made me feel like a rock star for a few seconds. I even gave drawing a try... I realized how talented and gifted most people are if only they could overcome their fears and tap into their creativity.

After dinner we went back to our last class which was from 6:00 p.m. to 9:00 p.m., then back to our rooms before lights out. It was extremely intense and it seemed pretty stressful at first. I wondered what it all had to do with being a missionary, but I soon found out. Given that I came directly from CFNI, my transition wasn't so difficult and I quickly adapted. The hardest part was being in a foreign country without my family, especially since I was used to having so many siblings around all my life. But it didn't take long for me to find my family there. On the weekends we would practice what we'd been taught and visit orphanages, nursing homes, and street kids. We tried to both entertain them and bring them a message of hope through our music and our skits. We loved doing it and they loved it too, so we made it part of our weekly routine.

My favorite place to visit though, was Boca Chica, an extremely poor island off the coast of Cartagena where we networked with other missionaries who were living there. They were building a school and an orphanage and we would go and assist them in their projects. The island had so much need. There was no running water, no electricity, and a scarcity of the simple and basic elements for living. The people lived in dirt shacks and fed on giant ants, fish, and lobster. Little black kids ran around naked in the dust-filled streets and played with sticks and rocks. It was in Boca Chica that I had an encounter which left me completely astounded. For me it was the confirmation I needed to know that I was in the perfect place at that time in my life.

I wasn't playing songs on my guitar with little children around me, and no, Boca Chica was not a communist Island. But on that island, 3,000 miles away from Dallas and 6,000 miles away from Romania, I met a girl. Her name was Daniela and she was living and working with the children of Boca Chica, providing medical assistance, and creating a better future for them. The divine coincidence was that Daniela was from Romania. I never expected to meet a Romanian in Cartagena, much less on this island. I couldn't believe it! And even more shocking was that she acted like she knew me.

"You look very familiar," she said with a witty smile. "Yeah, I'm not Colombian," was my retort. "Where are you from?" "Dallas," I replied. "But you are Romanian," she said, her eyes gazing away in deep thought. "Yes, I am." "Do you have a sister who has an orphanage home in Calarasi, close to Bucharest?" "Oh my dear God!" I exclaimed. "This is unreal!"

Well, it was, and she knew my sister whose name was also Daniela, as well as some of my other siblings from having worked with them at the Bethany House Project in Romania. She had left Romania to serve and provide humanitarian aid on this small island. I thought I had it difficult on mainland Cartagena, feeling like it was boot camp with limited food and being in class all day. Daniela was sleeping on dirt floors with the locals in peril of scorpion and snake bites. It was always hot and dry and there was no AC, television, king size beds, gourmet meals and the water needed to be purified. It was complete misery, but she loved it! She was transforming hearts and providing a better life for those people. She'd been there a good while and so much had been done already. There was also a couple from Mexico and a German who was overseeing the construction projects. "How long will you be here?" I asked. "Forever" she joked, "I don't know. This is very fulfilling."

She was a true missionary... What had compelled her to do this? What compels any of us to sacrifice our time, money, and energy to go out, help, serve, and love other people? For some it's compassion, for others it's an inner obligation, yet for others it's just a thrilling adventure. But no matter what your motive may be, it all requires some degree of love and humility. I learned there that this is what

Christianity is all about. It meant much more than being in a building hearing a sermon and singing a few nice songs. The essence of it all is going out and applying the teachings of Christ. These people were so thankful for what we were doing in the name of love. I was surprised at the joy I encountered in those slums. The misery and the filth some of these people lived in was beyond anything I had ever imagined, yet they were people like me and I knew they wanted more out of life. I learned a lot from them and again I was reminded of what a blessing it is to have the opportunity to live in the United States.

For three months we had the same schedule, but every day was unique. In those three months we got to know each other really well, and we became as bonded as a close-knit-community. We developed such a strong love for one another and the love began to manifest itself in the things we were doing. Many began to give away their nicer clothing to others who needed them more. Some shared their soap, shampoo, and toothpaste. When a student with some money would order a pizza they would share it with everyone else. Selfishness was losing and love was winning.

At the end of our three-month-missionary-boot-camp we were assigned to groups of fours and fives. We were going to spend our next two months in different cities or even different countries. I happened to be grouped with Karin from Norway, Cecy from Peru, and Jamie from Canada, and our mission field was going to be Cuba. Initially I wasn't too excited about Cuba because it meant being far from Alejandra. Plus I knew Cuba was communist and I wasn't that eager to visit a communist country having spent the first eight years of my life living in one. However, the more I thought about it, the more I knew I was supposed to go. The dream I had in Helsinki was being fulfilled.

14

❦

Cuba

(Memories of Monocracy)

The moment I set foot on Cuban soil I knew I was in another world. I felt as if I had been taken back in time by thirteen years. The airport personnel and security looked just like the communist soldiers of Romania and everything I saw within the first few hours reminded me of when I was a child behind the iron curtain. The heavy yoke of oppression and hopelessness I experienced in Romania was evident from the beginning. It was hard to imagine that America was a forty-five-minute boat ride away. Beyond the Gulf was another world. *"How can these people be subjugated to such a low life with hardly any opportunities and we being so close to them have it all?"* I asked myself.

I remember taking the taxi into Havana and watching as on each block there was a policeman monitoring what was going on. I had flashbacks of a day in Romania during the revolution when I came home after being in a nearby village with my mom for the weekend. There was no communication between villages, but we knew something was brewing. We just didn't know the revolution had begun. When we left home everything was calm, but when we returned the revolt had already spread from Timisoara and there were security forces all over our village watching and monitoring what was happening. Now here I was in Cuba after thirteen years of having experienced freedom and liberty, and the same feeling of oppression and despair haunted me. Although there were security forces all around me, I felt just as timid and insecure as in Romania when I was a child.

The streets of Havana were full of old American cars from the '40's, '50's and '60's that had been brought in prior to the Fidel take-over. In the center of the city was the Capitolio. It was basically a replica of the capitol building in D.C., but not as nice. It was one of the few places where tourists could use the Internet for $12 an hour, as long as their Cuban friends waited outside. Then there were the old, dirty, and broken-down buildings that were not maintained, falling apart, and in desperate need of renovation. The whole city's infrastructure needed a makeover.

We had to be careful of our every move, as the police kept a close watch on all tourists. On every corner they were taking notes of all that was happening. We waited until nightfall to go to the family that was hosting us since tourists were not allowed to stay with the locals and we needed to arrive without being spotted. It was a way for the communist government to control everyone who entered the country and where they stayed.

The Street-Walker

Despite the negative things I encountered, I soon realized that deep within me there was a unique attraction for Cuba and it didn't take long for me to fall in love with the Cuban people. They were jubilant and friendly and they loved ice cream, chess, dominoes, and cigars. Every day I would leave early in the morning to walk and take pictures of Havana.

One day I was in a small shop on a narrow road near the main tourist area looking for a gift to buy Alejandra.

As soon as I left the shop I heard a seductive voice, "Que me compraste papi?" I was too busy thinking about the little-white-Cuban-dress I just bought and how it would look on Alejandra, so without even turning my head I kept on walking.

Again the voice called, this time in English, "What did you buy me?" I turned my head slightly and a tall beautiful young lady was right behind me. "Oh," I said, shocked and intimidated by her stunning appearance. "First time in Cuba?" she asked with a softer and accented tone. "Yeah, first time," I replied in a hurry. "Do you love it?" She asked with an alluring smile as she took one step closer toward me. "Uh-oh," I thought, "this chick's trouble." I looked at my watch in distraction and said, "So far I like it, nice meeting you," and I smiled and walked away.

In what felt like a fraction of a second I experienced all these bizarre feelings, but deep inside I knew I had just escaped a snare. Just as I was untangling my thoughts, caught up in strange emotions set off by her vivid appearance, she grabbed me. Not in a rude disruptive way, it was more like a soft tap with her fingertips touching my chest.

She was too tempting to ignore, but I knew it was best for me to keep walking. She fired question after question, "Where are you from? Where are you staying? What is a handsome guy like you walking alone in Cuba?" I kept my answers short, but through her sense of humor and charm she managed to engage me in a conversation as we were now walking side by side.

"If I guess where you're from, will you stop?" "Maybe," I said. "France... Israel... Italy... Argentina..." "Argentina?" I interrupted, "...with this Spanish?" "Your appearance is more powerful than your accent," she responded.

"Alright, thanks for all the flattery, but I need to get somewhere," I said, as I turned toward Old Havana. "Where? Maybe I can help." She was relentless and quite intelligent for a streetwalker.

Now that I was entering the main square of Old Havana I figured she would shy away. Old Havana is full of shops, restaurants, galleries, museums, and people, locals and tourists alike. It was obvious that some of the locals knew her, by their reactions, but she didn't mind at all. In fact she blatantly offered her services to me as she caressed the back of my neck and told me how much she desired me.

"Nothing, you don't pay me... I just want to be with you." I was flabbergasted at how bold and shameless she was. "Honestly, I can't," I said, this time with a straight face. "I'm a missionary here in Cuba and I have a girlfriend." "And your girlfriend... is she here?" she questioned. "No, but it doesn't matter," I replied.

"She'll never know, just enjoy yourself, it's your vacation, have a little fun." "It's not only my girlfriend... I just can't," I said, as I entered an art gallery and that was the end of it. She walked away and I never saw her again.

I wish I could have talked to her to help her understand that she was worth more, or at least help her see that this lifestyle was destructive to her body and soul. There were many things I could have said, but I felt weak and somewhat insecure.

I also wished that Cuba could have had a better economy so women such as this one would not have to lower themselves to this extent and sell their bodies, but prostitution is one of the most ancient professions in the world, I reasoned. Still, I felt so saddened and frustrated.

I left the art gallery and continued my walking tour of Havana. I spent the rest of the day reading about Ernest "Che" Guevara and hearing the many ambiguous opinions held by Cubans about him. Some loved him, yet others said he was a murderer. I knew very little except that in Europe and certain places in America, he is glorified as being the true face of the revolution. My perception is that most people fell in love with the picture they saw and know little about who he really was.

The next day I went to the tobacco factory. I saw how they make the world's best cigars and realized that the same cigars, which were sold in the factory for four to five dollars, can be purchased on the black market for a fraction of the price.

Walking back towards Old Havana, I ran into a man who asked me where I was from. I told him Texas and he asked me to take him there. He basically begged me. "I have no future here, no job." "Why do you think I can help you?" I asked. "Because you look like a good American," he responded. "Actually, I was born in Romania and to a great extent I feel your pain." "But, honestly I don't know what I can do for you without jeopardizing my stay here." We continued talking until we arrived at a small cafe. I bought him a coffee and told him what Mom offered us while we were living under communist rule, "HOPE." I encouraged him to believe that a better life was possible and attainable. There was nothing left I could offer him, but he walked away believing...

In the coming days I would have repeated incidents of people asking me to help them escape to the United States. I truly felt blessed to live in freedom. I thought about how spoiled and lazy most of us in America have become. Many of the friends I grew up with were wasting away on drugs or alcohol. Some couldn't even maintain a simple job. But everyone felt a sense of entitlement... They believed it was the governments' job to take care of them and they were neglecting the numerous opportunities right in front of their eyes.

I would spend the next days wandering around Havana talking to the people and listening to their stories. I knew enough Spanish to hold a conversation with anyone. There was one specific art gallery which I frequented daily, talking to the owner and hearing his insight on art, communism, and life. His name was Cesar and he had a son named Roni who was always in the gallery with him.

They spent all day playing chess and smoking Cohibas. Most Cubans love chess and dominos and they are usually in the streets in their undershirts from early noon to evening playing and socializing. I loved their laid-back, worry-free lifestyle. I also loved to play chess and I would spend many hours at night playing chess with anyone who wanted to play. I just couldn't compete with the Cubans. I realized that after playing a ten-year-old-boy who beat me. After the humiliating loss I switched to playing dominos.

I felt like I was able to connect with the Cubans on a different level than the average tourist because I had once lived under the same tyranny that they were presently living under. Most Cubans hated Fidel Castro, the iron-fist dictator of Cuba. For over thirty years they had been under his rule and things had gradually gotten worse. They wanted a change, but like most Romanians prior to the Revolution, they were afraid.

I asked Cesar one day how the Cubans would respond if the United States would invade. He shrugged his shoulders and reached for a newspaper.

"See what it says? Cuba no es Iraq. It's the same tough government propaganda that we have been hearing for years." The article was about a possible attack on Cuba by the United States, fabricated by Castro's government to make him look like a fearless leader.

Apparently this wasn't anything new, but it was effective in rallying most people behind the tyrant. The Cuban people had no idea what was happening in the outside world and most of the stories coming from the state-owned-media were lies.

Rustic Encounters

It was now time for us to leave Havana and begin our real work. The first two weeks were more like a vacation than a mission trip, except for eating black beans and rice for breakfast, lunch, and dinner.

In the daytime I wandered around and at night we visited churches and shared the message of hope with them. Most churches were legal in Cuba, but under strict regulations and supervision by the government. If any of the state's rules are violated or if the church is perceived to be a threat to the state, it is immediately shut down and leaders could face fines and imprisonment. That was nothing new. Cuban communism or Chinese communism, when it comes to religious freedom, it's all the same.

We were headed to the country where most villages had no church buildings. They met in regular houses. We had no idea what we'd encounter in the country, but the biggest surprise was at the bus stop. The bus stops and routes are very spread out and people wait in line for hours, long hours to get anywhere. That day we waited for four-exhaustive-hours for the first bus. We were in a long single file line, which proved that this was an ordinary thing. Then, I realized why they wait for such a longtime. An eighteen-wheeler truck pulled up. The trailer was just like a regular trailer only with windows cut out on both sides. As soon as the bus arrived everyone jumped on like savages until the bus was completely full. This was our only option, and if we didn't get on this bus we were going to have to wait another four hours. Like nice tourists and missionaries we let people cut in front of us and get on the bus until there was no more room. The people were packed like sardines and there was just no way the four of us, my guitar, and our suitcases were going to fit, so we watched the bus leave.

As we waited for the next bus, an unusual lady, a bit creepy, with a long sad face, dressed in white clothes and carrying a black satchel, approached us. She was a practitioner of the Santeria religion, a faith I knew little about at the time. Apparently Santeria is an Afro-Cuban religion that started in Cuba with its roots in Nigeria. According to the people I spoke to, it is believed that the slaves imported to the Caribbean to work the sugar plantations had their own religious traditions, including a tradition of trance, animal sacrifice, and the practice of sacred drumming and dance.

She asked for something, but I couldn't understand what it was. It wasn't money, so I figured I should get her some food. "Un momento," I said as I ran across the street to an unmarked supermarket.

This was my first time in a local supermarket and I was shocked at what I discovered. There were no Snickers, M&M's or Doritos. There was no Gatorade or Red Bull. Yeah, there was Coca Cola, but it cost $4 for a twenty ounce bottle, because it was an America product. Their version of M&M's was "mani" which were peanuts in paper cones. So I bought the mani and some sugar-cane water for everyone and went back to the bus stop. The lady was gone. I asked Kathryn, our leader where she went. "I don't know she replied. "She kept asking who we were and where we were going." "Hmm," I thought. "Well, lets not make too much of it." I said, responding to what I perceived an uncanny moment. "Let's pray," Cecy suggested, as I tried to remain upbeat and optimistic. I didn't really have a good feeling about anything, but I tried not to worry the team by exposing my feelings.

After a total of eight hours the second eighteen-wheeler came and picked us up. It was just as full as the first, but this time we were determined to get on, missionaries or not. The bus took us close to the town where we were to spend our next ten days, but we were still a few kilometers away from our destination. The sun began to set, so we decided to walk instead of waiting for another bus. And walk we did, with all of our luggage on a long country road as night was dawning and the day was ending. There were fields of sugar canes to our left and to our right. Occasionally we would pass a house, a cow, or a farmer returning home after a hard day's work. I was getting very tired. I had my ovation guitar on my back, a suitcase, and a shoulder bag.

We walked and walked until a peasant in a straw hat with his horse and a flat cart stopped and asked us if we needed a lift. Since I was the only guy, I nodded my head and thanked him for his kindness. That was nice of him, but I wasn't sure this was better than walking. The carriage was practically falling apart and the road was bad and full of pot holes. After a while it got so dark that we couldn't see anything. There were no lights anywhere and we just had to trust this guy's goodness of heart and believe that he was taking us to the right town.

Mosquitoes had been devouring my skin all night and the wood of the cart pinched my skin. I was irritated, tired, and hungry, but like a good missionary I stayed positive and kept quiet. I felt somewhat responsible for the team's morale and I knew I needed to be a good role model.

When we finally arrived at the town, which consisted of forty houses or less, it was hard finding the house where we would be lodging. It was after midnight and we were starving and desperate to get some rest. After walking around for a while we located the blue house which matched the description of the house we were looking for. We were greeted by a middle aged woman with brown skin, long wavy hair, and a friendly smile. Her name was

Norma and she was Cuban. She welcomed us and offered us a drink.

The house was small, with two bedrooms, a living room where they had the church service, and a small kitchen. Norma was a widow, and the pastor who held the weekly services. She slept in one room and the girls slept in the other room. I slept on the concrete floor in the living room with a thin blanket under me. I felt strange and more out of place than ever and the deep silence, the pitch darkness, and the discomfort left me in need of spiritual assistance. After an hour or so of tossing and turning I prayed myself to sleep.

That night I had the spookiest dream. We were all sitting in the kitchen late at night getting ready for bed and suddenly there was a knock at the door. Norma quickly ran to see who it was. Before I could stop her, she had cracked open the door. The eerie guest was a tall dark woman with a long flat face dressed in black with evil eyes and a chilling ambiance. I woke up in a sweat. I didn't know what this dream meant, but I was quickly driven to my knees. It was our first night in this lonesome town in the middle of nowhere and there were no lights anywhere, no electricity, and all I could think about was that giant witchlike figure at the front door. It had been a bizarre day since the bus stop incident. I wondered if that lady at the bus stop had anything to do with my dream or was it just my fears. Was I creating my own nightmare or was there something more I needed to ponder? I knew doubting the mission wasn't an option, but the reality was that since leaving Havana our trip had become a struggle.

The next morning at breakfast I shared my dream with Norma and the team. They were all puzzled. Norma however, was even more puzzled. She looked at me and without saying a word, began pointing toward the sink, the ceiling, and the doors. She then asked, "Do you see why they are so high?" "No, why?" I curiously asked. She continued. "Before I moved here, there was no church in this town. This town is known for its voodoo practices and this house was where a witch once lived. She was very tall and that is why the sink, the door, and the ceilings are so high. She died about ten years ago from appendicitis. Then her daughter moved in and also died of appendicitis. Everyone said this house had been cursed. Finally, I moved in as a missionary pastor and before long I also had appendicitis and everyone thought that I was going to die, but miraculously I survived. There are still some people practicing voodoo around here so we must be cautious."

I was shocked by what I heard but I no longer felt frightened. What was this supposed to mean? It all started to make sense and I realized the spiritual significance was huge. "Let's pray for this town and for your stay here in Cuba," said Norma, "You guys are here on an assignment and no one will impede that."

Her faith encouraged all of us, but I couldn't help thinking about the nightmare. It wasn't necessarily a fear factor, but more a warning to keep us aware of what was taking place in this town. It was obvious that spiritual forces were active and the enemy didn't want us to have church in the home of a dead witch.

Every night twenty to thirty kids would gather at the house and we would sing, teach them theatre and mime, and enjoy many fun activities with them. We played games, taught them new songs, and read them stories from the Bible.

There was a song in particular, by the British group Delirious titled, "I Could Sing of Your Love Forever." This song was beautiful and it had been translated into almost every language. I would sing it in Romanian, Karin sang it in Norwegian, Jaime in English, and Cecy and the rest in Spanish. The kids had a blast with it as they tried singing along in every language.

Being there and loving these kids meant so much to them. Many of them had been abused, uncared for, and forgotten. They just needed someone to love them and to help them feel cared for. Within a week they were so attached to us that when it was time for us to leave many were crying and begging us to stay. We knew that we had touched their hearts and there was no doubt they had touched ours.

The next day we were packed and ready to leave the small town for yet another smaller town where we would be spending another week. As I sat there waiting patiently for the bus, car, or cart to take us to our next destination, I got my journal out and began writing.

We have been in Cuba for twenty-one days and I can feel a significant change in my life. We lead worship, preach, and minister every night. It's awesome. The electricity, if we even have that luxury, goes out every night, but that's OK. I realize that I can live without it. I realize now that I have been taking too many things for granted. It's so easy to get spoiled when you have everything. I am learning to appreciate small things, like water. We've also been doing a whole lot of walking and when we do get to ride it's not a taxi or a bus, it's usually a tractor or a horse carriage. Last night we went to a church which was literally in a barn, but it was so amazing. The people were so hungry for God. Then on the way home a rainstorm hit and we had to walk home in the rain. It was the longest walk.

A few weeks later I wrote.

My Journey in Cuba is winding down. I am ready for the city. We have been in the country for too long and it has been quite a struggle. We do so much walking every day. Our mission has been in the country, not in the city, and it has been extremely diffi-cult. The houses where we stay have pigs and chickens running around everywhere. Mosquitoes have eaten me all over. There is no electricity and water is very limited. Many times there isn't any and we have been doing our own laundry by hand. To top it off, I have to be on top of my game and ready to minister to these people under the additional pressure that I am doing it illegally. I don't feel enough freedom and sometimes I actually feel trapped as if in a cage. I can't wait to be in Romania with everyone. I miss home, my family, and Alejandra, especially when it rains, and it has been raining a lot. I know that I must stay strong, but it's just so hard right now.

It's pretty clear how things changed from week to week. Cuba was a difficult experience, but at the same time a very rewarding and eye opening experience. The price that I paid living in those conditions and giving myself to the Cuban people was very small compared to the joy, hope, and love that we shared together. I was once again reminded of the harshness of this life and my eyes were reopened to this forgotten reality that many people ever know. It was a reminder of my former life in Romania, and how quickly I had forgotten many of the hardships in my past. It taught me to cherish the life that I have in America and to be grateful that I was given the opportunity to live there.

I realized that I was only in Cuba for a short time, while these people live there all of their lives. That's all they have and ever will have. For someone like myself to come from a different country and try to spread a little cheer by sharing "the good news," singing a few songs, praying, or playing games at least gives them hope that there is more out there. It shows them that there is freedom and one day they can hope to encounter it. But more important was exposing them to the spiritual freedom that I've experienced. This was my purpose and my mission for going there and I have no doubt that it was accomplished.

15

Romania

(The Reunion)

It was so good for me to be back in Cartagena. It seemed like I had spent an eternity in Cuba. I was dying to see Alejandra and share all my experiences with here. I couldn't wait to get back and eat a good meal. Even McDonald's would seem like a delicacy after eating beans and rice for sixty days. But I was just so happy to see Alejandra and the rest of the students. Each of us had returned with our own stories and experiences.

As soon as I saw Alejandra my heart was ready to burst with joy out of my chest. We embraced each other like two long lost lovers who had been separated for years. "Baby, you lost so much weight," she said sympathetically. "And you're more gorgeous than ever," I replied. I was finally reunited with the beautiful Latina that I had left behind two months earlier. I came back with long hair and a beard and a bunch of dirty clothes. I looked like someone from "Survivor" and I felt like one too.

A few days later after completing our service, we packed up and hurried to Cali for the weekend, and from there to Europe. We had a busy and exciting summer ahead of us. It was mid-June and people were traveling again like never before. We would be flying from Cali all the way to Arad for a wedding. Following the wedding we were going to Toulouse, France to find a place for Alejandra and register for school.

As excited as I was to finally be going to my homeland with Alejandra, I was even more excited to see my entire family. It would be the first time since leaving Romania that the entire family would be reunited, and, ironically we would be reuniting for another wedding. Emilia, the first girl in our family also got married in Romania just before we left while Romania was still communist. Now it was Emanuel, the first Bistrian son to marry, but this time in a free Romania.

What a huge difference thirteen years in the United States of America made. We were all so thrilled about the monumental celebration because it meant so much for each one of us. It was the reunion of a life time, something we all had been longing for, for years. We would once again be together like in the days long gone, friends, neighbors, cousins, uncles, brothers and sisters. The only people that would be missing were my dear grandmothers.

This would be the most memorable celebration we'd experienced since leaving Romania.

Furthermore, to be able to celebrate a true Romanian wedding with the entire family made it all the more exciting. Just days earlier, I was in communist Cuba, reminiscing about communist Romania and dreaming of being back in the free world. I dined on black beans and rice for two entire months. Now I was ready for an unforgettable feast. Romanian weddings are enormous and very different from most American weddings. They typically last all day, and the food has to be exceptional or it cannot be a true Romanian wedding. There is usually a long ceremony that includes songs (choirs, orchestras, and symphonies), poetry, prayer, and preaching. But the fun starts with the reception.

The reception begins with a selection of appetizers that are so delicious, it's tempting not to stuff yourself all-at-once. Then there are the soups and a variety of meats accompanied by puree and pilaf. The people usually take long breaks, relaxing and socializing between the different courses, while the bride and groom go from table to table greeting the guests and taking pictures.

The final course is usually "sarmale," a typical Romanian dish. A Romanian wedding is not complete without the sarmale. There is a saying in Romania that when you eat good sarmale, "they're wedding sarmale." That's because bad sarmale on a wedding day can ruin the entire wedding. It's customary for everyone to stuff themselves, including the bride. Many people don't even eat breakfast on a wedding day. This is the one day that one can give in to their gluttonous appetites and not feel guilty. This wedding had it all and more…

Everyone enjoyed the festivities as much as the entire family enjoyed the celebration of the blissful reunion. We took more family pictures that day than we had taken in our lifetime. It was the first time that we could take a picture that included all twelve siblings. How delightful it was to have everyone together at last! The expressions on everyone's faces said it all. I looked at my parents who were sitting down, their faces displaying fulfillment and gratitude. For the first time in thirteen years their children were reunited. What a difference thirteen years in America had made! We left a hopeless village, empty handed, for a country where anyone can do anything, and though it was an uphill battle, we learned to succeed. The family was more united than ever and slowly, but surely, everyone was getting married and moving on with their lives.

Dad was having the time of his life being the proud patriarch of us all. He always carried a strong sense of pride, but this time it was more justifiable than ever. How could Dad not be proud? Proud of his great accomplishment, proud of the principles and virtues he and Mom had instilled in all of us, and proud to see his dreams being realized. It wasn't easy raising twelve children, especially in the conditions that they had to do it. Leaving behind everything they ever knew and going to a new country was both hard and daring. But they did a great job adapting to all the changes and they did a remarkable job raising all of us.

The most important lessons they taught us were done on a daily basis through the way they lived their lives, through their faith, hope, and courage, and their constant reminder to never forget our humble beginnings. That was their legacy then, and the legacy that will remain.

After thirteen years of living in America, the whole family was in a better place, happy, successful, and continuing to make progress in our lives, cities and families. The most difficult times were finally behind us and the future was growing brighter! We were finally living with the purpose that Mom constantly reminded us of when we were young kids living in Benesti.

As we sat there absorbing the last hours of this monumental celebration, sating our stomachs with wedding cake and other pastries, I walked over to where Mom, Dad, Uncle John, and Dad's sister were sitting. They were as merry as I've ever seen them. "Come sit with us," suggested my smiling Dad. I leaned over, took a sip of Mom's coffee and said, "This is really spectacular!" Mom's face gleamed with gratitude as she softly spoke, "Yes, we thank God for bringing us together after all these years."

That was the attitude Mom never ceased to display: "GRATITUDE." It's the one word that best describes her nature. Through the desperate times in the village, the difficult times in the first years in America, and through any circumstance, good or bad, she maintained her gratitude and hope for something better.

"As glorious as this may be, it falls short of the celebration to come," she said alluding to a Biblical passage read earlier.

"Let us rejoice and shout for joy! Let us celebrate and ascribe to Him glory and honor, for the marriage of the lamb, at last, has come, and his bride has prepared herself."

She never missed an opportunity to dream, to hope for a better life.

"It's so good to be together, just like old times, but better," I said. "Baba and Bunica are the only one's missing, but they're in a much better place rejoicing with us."

And so the testimony of God's mercy and favor was evident. And the legacy was just beginning...

"It's such a perfect day..." said Dad.

"And it's just the beginning of the Bistrian marriages," said my aunt.

"Next, it's you and Bonita," interrupted Uncle John, referring to Alejandra.

"We'll have to wait and see," I said with a plausible expression.

Epilogue

I n the coming years each of us would find our niche and settle down, whether in Romania or America. Daniela, the oldest, graduated college, married Dan (a native of California) and went back to Romania to start the Bethany Home Project. There she created a home for young girls who are kicked out of orphanages once they reach a certain age. Instead of these girls going to the streets to become prostitutes, she takes them in, trains and teaches them valuable trades, and helps them become successful young women.

Lidia and her husband left Chicago and moved to Knoxville, where they have a beautiful home and great careers. They also have two children who are in high school. Emily, the only one that remained in Romania when we came to the United States, is still running the family business with her husband in Ineu. They seem to be doing well, raising four biological children and a little girl they adopted.

Cornel graduated college and went back to Romania as a young missionary, serving the needs of our people. Within years he founded the Bible

College in Cluj-Napoca, the university center of Romania. Cornel met his wife there in Cluj. She was a student when they met. They now have a baby girl and a little boy. The school continues to do well and expand. The graduates are making a positive impact all over Romania and abroad.

Jenny and her husband Marius left their business and a beautiful home in Dallas to move to a town in Romania where there was great need. Together they started a church where they train and help young people find their purposes in life. They have three beautiful children. Peter is an electrician and has a successful business in Dallas, Texas. He married Nelly, a young girl from Transylvania. Together they continue the generous practice of making their home available to anyone needing a place to stay. They have two children and a third on the way.

Anna graduated college, went to massage therapy school, and became a masseuse. She is currently living in Dallas and dating Brian, another native of California. Emmanuel, along with his wife Bianca, moved to Romania to start an investment firm. They have two children. Danny and Abel, both college graduates, moved to Romania as well, working and serving at the Bible school in Cluj. Maria, my youngest sister, also graduated from Dallas Baptist University and married Jesse Santana from Los Angeles.

I would continue traveling the world, dating Alejandra and waiting patiently for the right time to "pop the question." I happened to do it over the Atlantic Ocean in a Boeing 777 from Paris to Atlanta.

It was a total surprise for Alejandra, considering she hadn't the slightest idea I was on that airplane. It was announced over the PA system by the pilot, since my request to do it myself was denied.

At 40,000 feet and almost an hour into the flight I heard my flawless and romantic script delivered by the captain. The next thing I remember, the airplane erupted in applause, and Alejandra awakened to total shock. I left my temporary coach seat, walked over to business class where she was, sat down in the empty seat next to her, and gave her the platinum ring I had purchased less than 24 hours ago, in Dallas.

Later that year we got married. She was twenty-one years old and I twenty-two. We had cross-cultural ceremonies in both Dallas and Cali, Colombia. Following our wedding we both went back to school to further our education. A few years later we founded the Light House Cultural Center, a place that encourages and supports young artists to use their creativity and imagination for the enhancement of our communities. We are currently living in Dallas with our two daughters, Ilona and Emma.

Mom and Dad continue to live in Knoxville, Tennessee in the same house we acquired through Habitat for Humanity. As of today, eight of their children have given them more than twenty grandchildren. They never miss an opportunity to visit Dallas, and ever since the reunion in 2003 they make an annual trip to Romania.

For more information about the Bistrian Family
visit www.bistrian.com

To know more about European American
Association and "The Light House" cultural center
go to www.eaadallas.org

And for autographed copies of Goodbye
Transylvania please visit
www.goodbyetransylvania.com

Acknowledgements

There are so many people that I would like to say thank you to, because without you my story would not be possible. In every phase of my life, beginning with Benesti, Chicago, Knoxville and Dallas there have always been people who supported and inspired me along the journey.

But I would first like to thank Jesus, my Redeemer, for giving me a purpose in life. My parents for giving me hope and inspiration, and for raising a family of warriors, even in the most difficult of circumstances, and to all my siblings for your love and unity. I also like to thank my wife Alejandra for her unwavering faith in me, and for being such a great mother to Ilona and Emma, my chocolate and my candy.

Many thanks to Israel Lambert for helping me believe by believing in me, for your support and your loyal friendship. To Jane Cross for all your help in editing this project, and the spontaneous encounter, that was no mere coincidence. To Michelle, Anita, Linda and Beverly (my NM buddies) for your tremendous assistance. I really value your input. To

Craig Nimphius, for editing and for all the encouragement you gave. To Mark Johnson for making the trips interesting. To Andres Cordova and Wade Issa for your ideas, your help, and your friendship. To Justin Daly for your Romanian humor. To Manu, Mara, and Neli for listening. To Melissa Bradley for your tender spirit and tenacity to finish the job, even after losing your phone because of me. And to all my CMH family because without those lonely winter nights in that boring apartment, this book would only be half written.

LaVergne, TN USA
28 January 2010
171542LV00001B/29/P